CHARLEMAGNE
AND THE
ADMIRAL OF SPAIN

A Carolingian cycle story adapted from translations of the
original 11th Century sources, including William Caxton's 1485
LYF OF THE NOBLE AND CRYSTEN PRYNCE CHARLES THE GRETE

SCOTT PAVELLE
AFTER
WILLIAM CAXTON

Published by Mugen Press
Pittsburgh, PA

Published by
Mugen Press
P.O. Box 11061
Pittsburgh, PA 15237, USA
www.mugenpress.com

Cover design: Miranda Pavelle

Interior illustrations: The block-print illustration of Fierabras in Chapter 7 is from the 1497 edition of Jehan Bagnyon's *Roman de Fierabras le Géant*. All other illustrations are drawn from the *Grand Chroniques de France*. Minor edits have been made for clarity and story continuity.

ISBN: 9781942920052

First Edition, August 2016

FOR KATE:
Ever and always for more reasons than
reason can count.

FOR MIRANDA:
Who gives us love, loyalty, and adventure, all in
one package.

AND FOR ELEANORE:
Who puts the song in our
Chansons de Vie.

WITH ADDED THANKS TO

WILLIAM CAXTON:
The father of English printing and an author whose works
have truly withstood the test of time. Lots and lots of time.

THE EARLY ENGLISH TEXT SOCIETY:
Without your labors, dedication, and publications over the
past two centuries this work would have been impossible.

A QUICK DISCLAIMER

You are holding a piece of medieval pulp fiction, with all the goods and bads that implies. I've included both parts in an effort to convey the true look-and-feel of the story. Bigotry ("By God!"-ing) was central to the narrator's and the characters' attitudes, motives and beliefs. It's all over the place. I cut out some when it got to the point of being gratuitous, but you'll find that plenty remains. Without it the story wouldn't be the same.

As for fairness and accuracy, they went right out the window – if you can say that when neither was around to begin with. For example: Islam is and always has been a rigidly monotheistic religion with an absolute ban on the consumption of alcohol. The "Saracens" in this book are idol-worshiping drunkards to a man. In a similar vein, words like "Pagan," "Heathen," "Saracen," "Moor" and "Turk" all have specific meanings, and only an ignorant, linguistic criminal would use them as interchangeable synonyms for "bad guy." I've used them that way nevertheless for the same reason I kept the over-the-top bigotry. Those elements are as essential to the story's "feel" as the hard-drinking idolaters.

For what it's worth, the Christians are no better when judged by modern standards. They murder women and children just as eagerly as the Saracens do. As I see it there are two ways to explain this: First, that kind of behavior may simply reflect what was normal and accepted in the medieval point of view, with "good" and "bad" being defined by whose ox was getting gored rather than the nature of a particular act. That's the *"It's good when we do it to you, but bad when you do it to us,"* interpretation. Or we might be looking at a subtle social commentary by the original authors. I guarantee there was more than a little of that going on, because there's a lot of anti-superstition rhetoric that did not originate with me, and reads just as easily as a condemnation of blind faith in any kind of supernatural viewpoint. Either way it is another thing I left undisturbed in my attempt to convey the story using modern words.

Here's the bottom line folks. There are more mistakes and slanders in here than anyone could count. Those mistakes say more about the original authors and their world than they do about anyone who got slandered. Getting offended as a modern reader would say more about you than it does about them.

So sit back and enjoy the rollick without obsessing over its warts.

CLICK HERE TO ACCEPT **(Just kidding)**

CHARLEMAGNE
AND THE
ADMIRAL OF SPAIN

A cycle story from the Carolingian saga
By Scott Pavelle

TABLE OF CONTENTS

Chapter

INTRODUCTION

What you're holding is a mixture of *adaptation* and outright *retelling*, not a *translation*. Those are wonderfully plastic distinctions that cover a multitude of sins. This Introduction explains a few of the biggest, along with why I made them. See the Afterword and the Chapter Notes if you want to know more about the actual details.

First question: Why not stick to the words as written? There's one and only one reason: I wanted to tell this story in a way that would entertain the modern reader. If doing so required deletions, additions, or changes, I did so without compunction. If it needed new chapters, I did that too. If the syntax was fine I left it alone, but where it failed to flow for the modern ear I made changes as I saw fit. The goal was to translate the essential part of the story – the emotional message – into words and scenes that would move a modern heart. That is, in my opinion, the truest core of the story itself and that's what I wanted to convey. It's as simple (and far reaching) as that. Nothing in the originals was sacred writ.

What specific parts were deleted or changed? For starters, a good bit of material that dealt with pedigrees, some extraordinarily long physical descriptions, and similar bits of detail. Medieval audiences seem to have loved that kind of thing but it drove me crazy. I also trimmed the religious bigotry down to a bare minimum and did my best to misuse all the "exotic" names (pagan, heathen, Turk, etc.) in a roughly equal and over-the-top way.

What was kept? The essential plotline with all of its elements. Like all good stories, the Charlemagne romances are about the central characters and how they interact with each other and their exciting situations. If I've done my job right, you'll get the same thrills and laughs that our ancestors did when these stories were new and current a thousand years ago.

About the Carolingian Cycle

"Cycle stories" are families of interrelated tales, poems and songs composed and retold by hundreds of different people and featuring a common set of characters and stock assumptions. They permeated the Middle Ages, reaching their best-known heights in the French tales about Charlemagne and the English tales of King Arthur. Each cycle has many dozens (probably hundreds) of individual pieces. They aren't really "episodes" because each one stands alone. A closer analogy might be fan fiction – a long series of sequels, prequels, and sideways excursions created by a variety of authors with no one but the audience to complain about inconsistencies.

For example, Roland's origin varies in different stories from the bastard love-child of Charlemagne's sister who was born and raised in a cave (that's my favorite), to the son of the Duke of Milan. On the other hand, Roland is always referred to as Charlemagne's nephew, and every version specifies that he knew Oliver as a boy. A storyteller had wiggle room when it came to more obscure events like how the pair came to be friends in their youth, but his audience wouldn't permit anything that changed the fixed poles of the cycle itself.

This book is woven together from several cycle stories that related a series of connected (or connectable) events.

If you want to read this in the spirit of your ancestors who got to hear it, take a moment to remember all the other stories about Charlemagne and his knights that you chanced on over the years. For example, did you ever hear the story called *"A Roland for an Oliver"*? It starts with a war between a relatively young version of Charlemagne and his rebellious Duke of Vienne, a city on the Rhone River in southeast France. The rulers agreed to settle their dispute in a duel of champions. Charlemagne sent his nephew Roland, who he was sure would win. The Duke of Vienne sent a young knight who had just arrived at his court and promptly bested all of the Duke's other men. His name was Oliver. The two young men went at it dressed in new armor with face-covering great helms. The epic struggle started at dawn and continued without pause until the sun was low, with neither man able to gain an advantage. Then Oliver's sword shattered at the exact same moment when Roland's caught in a crack of his opponent's shield. Deprived of their weapons, the two fell to wrestling. Once again they were so evenly matched that their helms popped off at the exact same moment.

The boyhood friends and recognized each other instantly, and turned to hugs and tears instead of blows. Taught by this example, the King and the Duke made their peace, and turned their efforts to the common foe. But that's a tale for another day...

Everybody knew some version of *"A Roland for an Oliver."* It informed their view of the characters when they heard some version of the story you're now holding. Now you have the same bit of background.

Here's another: Roland and Oliver were inseparable comrades until the moment they died together in the *"Song of Roland"* as victims of Ganelon's treason – the sort of intimate, unbreakable friendship that doesn't exist in today's world because of the way we twist all things to be about sex. I'm not giving anything away by telling you that. In fact, the stories are built on the assumption that you, the audience, know about that ultimate ending even as you are listening to this particular tale of something that came before.

The Arthurian cycle has a very similar structure with a totally different set of characters, events, and established "facts." For a parallel example, imagine you were a medieval storyteller and wanted to tell of

Lancelot's youth. You'd have some room to wander, but only within the rules established by the stories your audience already knew. Your version of young Lancelot may be kind, cruel, proud, or petty, but he must grow up somewhere in France, prove to be a prodigy of arms, and end up going to Camelot in service to Arthur's dream.

The experts seem to agree that there are more stories in Carolingian cycle than the Arthurian one, despite the fact that Camelot has a much greater penetration into modern America. In some ways the two cycles are very similar. Both center on grand arcs of triumph and tragedy, albeit with different flavors. The treason of Ganelon is a central theme in the Charlemagne stories, for example, while the love triangle of Arthur, Guinevere, and Lancelot is essential to Camelot.

But it's not really about the events when you come right down to it. The joy of these stories is as much about visiting with old friends as it is in hearing a new adventure. If you enjoy this one, go look up some others.

How Corny Can You Get?

That depends on how you define the term. The stories in this book didn't come from authors who drew on clichés. These images and adventures are the origin – the sun source – of all those scenes of heroic knights and lovely maidens that became the clichés. The stories only became corny as a result of over exposure. Consider: What line could be triter than, *"To be or not to be, that is the question?"* The answer is: nothing, unless you're reading Hamlet itself. Same thing here.

TABLE OF CHARACTERS

The stories in the Carolingian Cycle (from "Carolus," the Latin form of Charles) range from serious and eternal works of literary art to the medieval equivalent of light fiction. This particular story falls in the second category. It isn't about grand themes and philosophical questions. It's an excuse to visit with old friends and enemies. This should help you keep track.

Aloys   The evil cousin whose scheming caused Ganelon's fall. Here is the *real* villain of the piece, a scoundrel we can really love to hate. It's no coincidence that he appears in the later adventures as the bosom friend of Charlemagne's unworthy son.

Astrogot   The giant King of Ethiopia. He is the biggest and strongest of all his race, and bears a dreaded, solid iron mace is longer than a man is tall and shaped at the top like the head of a full-grown boar. Astrogot can crush even the strongest knight to jelly with a single blow from that mace, and there aren't many knights who can face him without turning to jelly by themselves.

Aubrey   The eldest son of Duke Basyn.

Aimery   The son of Duke Hernaut and a 1st cousin of Oliver. Those in the know will recognize him as the future conqueror of Narbonne in a well-known story that takes place soon after the disaster at Roncesvalles. If you're really and truly up on the subject you'll know Aimery's grandfather too (Garin de Monglane) and his son (Guilluame d'Orange, not to be confused with the hundreds-of-years later William of Orange who became the king of England). They all have *chansons* of their own if you care to look them up.

Balan   The Admiral (*i.e.*, Emir) of Spain, Sultan of Baghdad, and master of other broad lands including the invincible town and bridge of Mantryble, the great walled city of Aygremore, and pretty much any other famous land you care to name between Hither and Yon. His people seem to like him well enough despite a bad habit of foaming, spitting, and turning colors when our heroes defy him. Balan is also the nephew of King Corsuble, the father of Fierabras and Floripas, and the uncle of both King Clarion and Galafer of the Mantryble bridge.

Basyn   The Duke of Bordeaux, a Paladin, and Aubrey's father. (For the sake of continuity, I like to think he's also the father of Huon, who stars in his own epic set ten or fifteen years later but was too young to join in this one).

Brullant   A Moorish king in fealty to Balan. This is the one to worry about – clever, loyal, brave and even a little wise. If only he were on the right side...

Charlemagne ("Charles the Great")   Oddly enough, the historical King of the Franks and Emperor of the West often turns out to be a greater and more likeable man than the legend who appears in these stories. The real Charlemagne earned the title of "great" with a serious of astonishing deeds and triumphs that are well worth looking into if history's your thing. The one in the stories is harder to rate. Indeed, he does so much wrong and so much right that it's almost an impossible task. He wounds those who love him uncountable times, but he's great enough to heal them. He swears rash oaths but he's great enough to keep them. He makes rash, impulsive decisions that only later events reveal as key foundations for God's greater goals (which are carefully and explicitly revealed, of course). Above all, Charlemagne's strengths are so great they become his flaws, but he draws (and can trust) men of so high a caliber that his flaws are concealed – until the disaster at Roncesvalles will deprive him of that crutch. And, of course, Charlemagne is the only one whose vision is so clear and so long that we know it endured to inspire an Age.

Clarion   The nephew of Balan and a brother-king of Brullant and Sortibrant. A famous knight in his own right, he has a champion named Rampyr who's even more dangerous. He owns a famous magic saddle that makes all of his steeds better than any other horse in the world (except Bayard of course, but he and his master appear in a different tale).

Coldroe   Another Saracen who's a good fighter but doesn't know when to keep quiet.

Cornyfer   A king of the Turks who captains an elite troop of 5,000 seasoned warriors. A sneak and a dastard like all the Turks, he finds out the hard way that 5,000 is not enough when Roland's on the other side.

Corsuble   The Uncle and primary general of Admiral Balan. He's been around long enough to forget more about the art of war than you ever learned, and then to write the book that you studied to learn it.

Cortana   The sword of Ogier the Dane.

Durandal   The sword born by Roland.

Fierabras   A magnificent giant who is the son of the Admiral of Spain. His name translates as "iron arm." Fierabras is the ultimate Saracen; a puissant and noble knight whose only real flaw is fighting for the wrong side.

Floripas   The daughter of Balan and the sister of Fierabras. Wealthy, witty and wise in the ways of magic and herbs, she's also a famous beauty with a clever mind – at least for a woman (read on and you'll get it). During the Saracens' sack of Rome she fell in love from afar with the young Guy of Burgundy. I wouldn't rejoice too fast if I were you, Guy.

Galafer   A fierce but not-too-bright giant who guards the invincible Mantryble Bridge. He's a nephew of Admiral Balan.

Ganelon of   The traitor who will eventually plan the doom of so
Mayence   many heroes at Roncesvalles and thereby prevent the conquest of Spain. But... Treason wouldn't hurt so much if the traitor wasn't both loved, and deserving of that love. Like Benedict Arnold in later days, Ganelon began as a hero. He *earned* the trust he betrayed. In this adventure we see him before the fall, and it's as poignant a scene as anyone could wish. He's not just a Paladin, he's a *great* Paladin. At one point in this story his feats bring even Roland to tears and move Oliver to say, *"May God preserve him, brother, I love the man with all my heart. Save you and Charles, there's none I love any better."*

Great as he may be, though, we know what happens in the end. Ganelon's name *meant* treason for the better part of a thousand years. Neither "Charles the Great" nor "Ganelon the Traitor" can ever escape the verdict that goes with their names.

In fact, the looming shadow of the *"Song of Roland"* pervades a great many of the cycle stories, this one included. The clues are sprinkled with a heavy hand; the seeds of treason all too clear to see. Ganelon never hears of Oliver's words, for example, far less of Roland's tears. If only he'd known how they truly felt... In another scene Aloys insists they leave the King for dead. "Who would ever know?" Ganelon refuses contemptuously, and ends up leading the charge that saved Charles' life. But he never reveals what Aloys' wanted, and he did pause to listen.

Above all, we see at work the acid that will ultimately wear the stone away: Ganelon resents the way Charles overlooks him, takes him for granted, and heaps all the praise on Roland. Make no mistake – the King is wrong in this. Ganelon earned that praise, and the King is supposed to give it. There are many reasons he fails to do so. Some we can even understand. But the fact remains that it doesn't get done. All it would take is a timely word – we *know* that – but the end is preordained, the fate is sealed, and we can't reach inside to make it right. That's why they call it "tragedy".

Geoffrey	A knight of Anjou and a Paladin.
Gerard of Montdidier	A Paladin, the son of Duke Thierry, and a very good friend to Oliver when he really needs one.
Guy of Burgundy	A younger Paladin and Roland's cousin. Floripas likes him more than he might wish.
Hernaut	The noblest hero of Rome, and a brother to Duke Reyner of Atri (Oliver's father). Reyner is the actual ruler of Atri and a direct vassal of Charlemagne, while Hernaut is "merely" the leading citizen of Rome and the captain of its defense.
Hautclere	Oliver's famous sword.
Iblis	Balan's favorite court knight, the King of Samarkand, and the promised husband of Floripas. Do you think his name is a coincidence? If so you need to bone up on your Arabic.
Joyeuse	The sword of King Charles.
Mambrino	A giant king of the Moors who owns a magic helmet and scorns the use of any blade. Not the brightest star in the sky, but he doesn't need to be. Invulnerability is a nice trick when you can manage to pull it off.
Maradas	A Moorish King and champion. He never learned that introductions should come *before* the battle.

Maragonde	Floripas' maid, who converted to Islam to save her life. Fat chance.
Mephistus	An enchanter hired by the Admiral of Spain to burn the Paladins out of their Tower retreat. He did fine with the men but forgot about the women.
Mervyn the Thief	A man of wondrous talents who never learned the lesson about "two in the bush."
Duke Naymon of Bavaria	The King may speak with God, but it's Naymon who sees through the cloudy world of men. He is Charlemagne's best friend, truest advisor, and the only one who can say what the King doesn't want to hear and nevertheless get heard. But that's not his only worth. Naymon may be old and gray but he's still a man among men.
Ogier the Dane	Ogier is the national hero of Denmark to this very day. His evil stepmother delivered him as a hostage to Charlemagne's court, and then caused his father to break an oath to the King, hoping to get the lad slaughtered in accordance with law. Even as a boy, however, Ogier's character shined like the springtime sun that wakens the sleeping earth with a kiss. Wise Duke Naymon intervened and took the boy under his wing. The tale of Ogier and Charlemagne came to a tragic end, but that's a tale for another day. He ended up ruling at home and is the Danish version of 'The King Who Will Come Again.'
	In the spirit of 'truth is stranger than fiction,' have a look at the origins of history's most famous knight: William Marshal, the man who taught Richard the Lionheart how to fight. King Stephen took Young William as a hostage, but his father refused to treat for his life. "I can always make another son," was the answer. The boy's courage was so impressive, however, that Stephen hadn't the heart to kill him. And the rest, as they say, is history. The King certainly knew the tale of Ogier.

One can't help but wonder if it didn't play a part in Stephen's decision. The eerie thing is, you could draw many more parallels if you chose to look.

Oliver
Roland's inseparable comrade is all that his friend is not, and all that we hope to be: the purified essence of Chivalry. He's also the conscience that keeps Roland human. It's no coincidence that Roland didn't die of wounds alone at Roncesvalles – he died of a broken heart when he discovered that he'd managed to get Oliver killed.

Paladins, The
The Paladins a/k/a the "Twelve Peers" ("Dozperes") are Charlemagne's champions; his equivalent of Arthur's knights of the round table. The various stories list far more than twelve, but that's a solvable problem if you assume there were only twelve at any given time. Some of the stories seem to violate that rule as well, but *c'est la vie*. It's no doubt the result of medieval spellcheckers.

Plourance
The most famous of Fierabras' three swords.

Pope, The
Why are you asking? He's the Pope, not a person! What, were you expecting some kind of actual facts or history? Good luck with that.

Rampyr
The champion of King Clarion (see above).

Reyner
The Duke of Genoa and Atri, Oliver's father, and the savior who gave food to Roland's mother when she hid for her life in a cave. (But that's another – well, you get the idea).

Richard of Normandy
The Duke of Normandy and a senior Paladin. A doughty fighter and the greatest horseman of the age.

Roland
The greatest knight in the world, but not one of the easiest to get along with. Roland is passionate, headstrong, loyal, blunt, and so arrogant that he'd have died long ago if he wasn't in a class of his own. He's the sort of hero who will happily charge

a thousand foes when everyone else is sure it's suicide. The heck of it is, he's right. When the enemy sees him coming they start to think, *"He wouldn't do this if he didn't have some edge."* That makes them hesitate until he's close enough for sword work. Bad Mistake. With Durandal in hand Roland starts to send heads flying "like quail rising up from a field." Before long, the 950 who remain start to think, *"Maybe I'll let someone else handle this..."* When Oliver hits from another side, their panic and doom are writ in the stars. *"For never did the sparrow flee from the hawk like the heathen ran from Roland."*

Sortibrant   Another king in fealty to Balan. He's not very nice, but he is very clever – just ask him. A loyal follower of the various heathen gods.

Tenebres   The brother of King Sortibrant. You'd have thought with all those Paladins caught in the Tower a man could be safe, but nooooo...

Thierry   The Duke of Ardennes and one of the more famous Paladins.

Twelve Peers   See "Paladins."

William the Scot   Another heroic paladin.

THE KNIGHTS IN THE TOWER

Captives	*Rescuers*
Duke Basyn of Bordeaux	Aubrey of Bordeaux
Geoffrey of Anjou	Guy of Burgundy
Gerard of Montdidier	Duke Naymon of Bavaria
Oliver	Ogier the Dane
William the Scot	Duke Richard of Normandy
	Roland
	Duke Thierry of Ardennes

SARACENS OF NOTE

Admiral Balan

Fierabras, King of Alexandria

Floripas, who needs no title

Corsuble, a King and more

Iblis, King of Ethiopia

Sortibrant, King and Counselor

Brullant, a Moorish King

Clarion, a Moorish King

Rampyr, a Champion

Astrogot, a Giant

Mambrino, a Giant

Galafer, a Giant

Mephistus, the Enchanter

Mervyn, the Thief

CHAPTER 1 – THE INVASION OF ROME

It befell toward the end of March, when field and stream wax gay and courage begins to prick, that Balan, the Sultan of Babylon and Admiral of Spain, set off to the greening wood to chase the boar and bear. Anon he grew weary and sought rest beneath a holly tree. It was there he received word that pirates had seized a rich ship bound from Babylon. The messenger seemed close to tears.

"A thousand pounds of pearls and precious stones, Sire! Spices, oil, silver, and brass! The treasure had been gathered in quantity as tribute from Your eastern lands. Now all of it is gone and the crew slain, save for a single sailor who lived to tell the tale."

"Where was this?" asked Balan. "And how came the sailor to survive?"

"It was the Romans again, Your Majesty. Those waters are as perilous as any in the world. The pirates grow bolder with each passing year, but their Pope refuses to do anything about it."

"And the sailor?"

"He was captured through no fault of his own – struck into the sea and taken while his senses were still confounded. To save his life he converted to Christianity and promised to serve in the hall of the Pope. As soon as the Romans eased their guard he escaped instead. Then he came straight here to bring you this word in hope of a golden reward."

"Give him the reward he earned," said the Admiral. "Melt a hundredweight of gold and pour it down his treacherous throat. Any man who'd betray our gods, even in empty words, deserves no better!"

Balan turned to his son Fierabras once the messenger was gone. Whatever may be said of the Admiral himself, Fierabras was justly accounted as the most marvelous giant in all the world. Though most men barely reached his chest, and very few stood as high as his shoulder, Fierabras was perfectly formed in every way. His skin was dark as the sea at night, his eyes glittered like stars, and his features were so even and well shaped that angels might have sighed with delight.

"Fierabras, we have conquered in Asia, Africa, Russia, and Spain. It is time we added Europe as well. If their Pope cannot control his own seas we shall start at Rome. May our gods Mahon, Mars and Apollo send me to die as a beggar if we do not dine from the throne of St. Peter ere the summer sun is high!

"Assemble your armies from Alexandria and Syria and have them ready to march anon. Also send word to King Iblis of Samarkand to supply us with both ships and the fiercest of his Turkish levies. Send too to the brothers Clarion and Brullant who rule so much of Spain. I will expect from each at least 100,000 men. A single soul less and I'll have their heads on pikes!"

The Admiral continued thus for several minutes, detailing both the levies he demanded and the tasks for their kings and princes to perform. Heathen though he was, Balan knew well how to conquer a country. By June a great array of carracks, galleys and other noble ships had gathered together by Aygremore, with a drummond for the Sultan and his lovely daughter Floripas. Two idols sat on high seats in the maintop, surrounded by severed heads to menace the Christians by their example.

Every ship in the fleet bore sails made from fine red silk embroidered with fantastical beasts and birds, and every flag and pennon boasted the Sultan's arms – four gold lions on a field of azure blue. Admiral Balan spared a moment to soak in this mighty display and then called out to the assembled men.

"First We shall see to the destruction of Rome! Then We shall move on to Charlemagne! Today I give you my vow: the Emperor of France shall bend his knee to kiss Our feet, or adorn Our gates with his head!"

A cheer went up and then the fleet set sail. Aided by generous winds they came to the ports by Rome without a hint of warning. Many a grim man landed, and many a town, abbey and church they burned to the ground. Uncountable souls woke in the morning unworried only to find their deaths ere the sun was low.

The heathen seemed unstoppable.

TIDINGS of the invasion came quickly to Rome. The Pope sent out panicked notes to summon his council. The moment they arrived he bleated, "The Sultan of Babylon has come to steal our treasures and sack our stores! He burns and destroys our people even now. Scarcely a one has been left alive. Saint Peter be our guide and save this worthy city!"

These rumors frightened the council no less than the Pope. At length one of the senators raised his voice above the din. "We cannot hope to defend against so mighty a host. We must send word to Charles, that noble King of beloved France. Only he could hope to save us!"

"No!" said Duke Hernaut, a bold knight who'd lately been made a Senator as well. "Our heads are yet whole, our shields intact, and our armor, spears, and swords are untested. If we send to Charles without attempting our own defense, what could we possibly win? Only the villainy that falls to all cowards! He would henceforth treat all of Rome – City and Church alike – as naught but the most craven of vassals.

"As yet we know nothing but rumor of this Admiral and his armies; and rumor is like a fisherman who sits down to drink with his friends. Ere the first cup he had a net of mackerel; by the last it's grown to a string of whales." He paused a moment to look around the hall, meeting each man's gaze directly. Then he continued: "I do not say we should treat this lightly. Not at all. But I do say we should deal with it ourselves until our own eyes have seen the truth. Give me ten thousand men to test this foe with spear and shield. Then we may decide what to do in a manner that befits our fathers."

The other senators bowed their heads to both the dignity of the man and the honor of his words.

SO IT CAME to pass that the next day saw Duke Hernaut riding forth from the city walls to challenge the heathen's approach, armed in steel and accompanied by the boldest bachelors that Rome had to offer. His son Sir Aimery, who was universally accounted as the best of them all, rode by his side. Hernaut called to this host from high in the saddle as the city gates opened up before them.

"My friends and comrades! Today we will prove that the ancient blood of all-conquering Rome can still be found inside her walls. Show yourselves worthy and we shall return this evening in triumph!"

The band rode forth with eager hearts, but soon discovered that rumor had not overstated the tales of ruin and death. A fell and angry silence replaced the laughter and cheers.

The path of burning and devastation led them directly to what seemed like a city of Saracen tents. Unlike the heathen, however, they had no benefit of surprise. Balan's Uncle Corsuble, wise with half a century's experience at war, had left spies and scouts out in all directions. This meant that Fierabras was prepared and waiting when Hernaut's troop had barely come in sight of the enemy camp.

The mere sight of this Saracen prince had been known to render many men speechless with awe. Standing afoot he would have towered over most like they did over a half-grown boy. Mounted and armed for war... It was enough to set even the stoutest heart atremble.

It began with the huge stallion on which he rode: the choice of two continents, twice the size of a normal charger, blacker than darkest night, and trained to be even deadlier than his master to a man on foot. Both knight and steed wore black armor the same shade as the giant's skin, crafted from ten thousand adamantine scales gilded at every edge and inscribed with prayers to his god Mahon that made them harder than the finest steel. The saddle and harness were likewise black, as was all his other gear save the helm, which glittered with precious gems.

He also bore three swords at his side, each more splendid than the last. The first came from a king he'd slain in India, the second from a king in Russia, and the third he'd won on a quest. This last bore the name of Plourance and came from the hand of Agnisiax the Smith, whose brothers had made Roland's sword Durandal, Charlemagne's Joyeuse, Ogier the Dane's Cortana, and Oliver's famous Hautclere. The giant's shield was likewise a thing of marvelous strength: crafted of steel, banded with iron, and adorned with a painting of his god Apollo.

Withal, he seemed more like a figure from a story than one who walks the actual earth. But real he was and just as puissant in combat as he was in his display. It was this figure of daunting perfection – with arms the size of most mens' thighs and thighs the size of chests – who sprang out to meet the Romans with fifteen thousand Moors at his back.

The struggle that followed was fierce, strong, and endured for many hours. More than once the courage of the Romans claimed an advantage at various parts of the field, but they could not win the battle because none could stand against Fierabras himself. The giant heathen led charge after charge, shattering the Roman lines and lending heart to their foe just as victory seemed most sure.

At one point Fierabras came to duel with young Aimery. A sort of odd peace descended around them as every eye fixed on the titanic battle. The clash of blade on blade sounded like twenty smiths at the forge, and sparks filled the air like stars in the sky. The two exchanged unceasing blows for so long that men began to wonder if they'd somehow stumbled into a dream. It finally ended when Aimery's warhorse stepped on a broken blade that stabbed the soft meat of its hoof. The beast screamed with shock and pain, rising up and pawing at the air. Fierabras struck back at the horse by sheer reflex, cutting clean through its neck despite a heavy coat of plate barding. It collapsed in place, pinning Aimery to the ground.

Fierabras towered above him for a moment – giant man on monstrous mount – and then saluted his fallen foe from the saddle.

"You are too fine a knight to be slain for such a mischance, young man. You have my parole until we fight another day – on one condition. Bear this message to whoever leads your defense:

"The cause you fight for is hopeless. My father the Admiral of Spain comes hither with more soldiers than there are grains of sand on yonder beach. Surrender the city and I swear to protect you all. You shall be my captives and no other's, shielded by my honor. Resist, and you will face destruction. Resist, and the entire population of your city, from the mightiest knight to the smallest child, shall be slain or sold into slavery. Resist, and all you love shall be doomed.

"Tell your Pope what I have done. Tell him what I have said. Tell him to choose wisely. And fare thee well, until we cross blades again!"

The fight continued after that for perhaps an hour, until a cry went up from the Christians closest to shore. "Ships! A thousand ships are coming toward land beneath the heathen flag!"

The sight sent a wave of fear through Hernaut's men. The Duke himself could only stare aghast at the uncountable number of sails closing in, and the armies such an armada would contain. He sounded a horn to call the retreat before enemy reinforcements could land. Ten thousand Saracens lay dead or maimed on the mud and grass, but the Romans too had been badly mauled. And their intelligence of the days to come was terrifying.

"WE HAVE upheld our honor," Duke Hernaut told the Pope and Senate that night. "We have met the foe in battle. We can report truly on his strength, that he is a foe beyond our means. Only the combined hands of all Christian men can hope to resist this heathen tide. Was it not I who counseled patience before, when we faced only rumor? So my words tonight should bear extra weight: We must send to King Charles!

"I will write the letter myself if you ask. My brother, Duke Reyner of Atri, sits on the royal counsel and my nephew Oliver is one of the King's favorite knights. They will listen and confirm that my word is good. The King *will* ride to our aid."

The plea fell on deaf ears. A phantom army had sent the priests into a panic, but now the enemy had turned into actual men. And real men with real swords – however numerous – scared the rulers of Rome much less than the fears conjured up from their own imaginations.

"The cost would be too high," answered one of the Vatican cardinals. "If Charlemagne comes to our rescue he may well demand that we pay for his war. We have worked too long and too hard enriching our coffers to take such a risk! Let Your Holiness call for a crusade instead. That will make it every man's Christian duty to battle the heathen wherever they might be found. Who can doubt that King Charles will approve? When we let it out – in a month, or perhaps two – that this Admiral has conveniently arrived in Italy itself, his own words will force the Emperor to ride against the enemy. Since it won't happen in response to a plea from us we will gain his help just the same, and he shall be obliged to thank us for the chance rather than asking us to pay."

Duke Hernaut demanded, "What good is treasure when your home has been burned and your children sold into slavery? You heard the message borne by my son. Aimery is a mighty man for all his youth. It has been years since even I could overthrow him in practice or joust. A knight who could meet Aimery in fair combat – let alone make a claim to victory – is an enemy who commands our respect. This is no rabble coming! It is a force to be feared."

"Pfaugh," said one of the Senators, "there speaks a father's pride. Besides, from the way you tell it your son only lost due to an accident. This isn't your coin, Your Grace, it is ours! Surely we who earned the gold have the right to spend it as we desire."

The Cardinal adjusted his heavy robes and then added, "Your lack of faith in Christian arms smacks to me of sacrilege. Do you doubt in the strength of Our Lord? God and his angels would never allow heathens to enter the city of St. Peter! You should do penance for even thinking such a thought."

In the end the Pope elected to side with his bishops and bankers. He sent priests streaming out in all directions to raise the banner of holy crusade, with orders to speak never a word of the devils that threatened Rome itself. At the same time he personally begged Hernaut to stay and take charge of the city's defense.

"I understand your frustration, Your Grace. I really do. But the counsel's arguments compel me to take their part. Word shall go out to King Charles on the ides of August. That is the day when Our Lord took the Blessed Virgin to join him in heaven. What could be a more auspicious moment to invite King Charles to join the battle for Rome? In this matter you must be ruled by Our decree. In all other things, however, the command of the city shall be yours. Every lay hand shall move as you direct: knights, militia, and commoners alike. Not a woman shall cook nor a child play in the street save in service to your desire."

The Duke could only bow his head before the king of the Church, but there can be no denying the bitterness in his tone when he quoted the Pope's words to his son that evening. Young Aimery exploded with frustration.

"*'Compelling reasons?'* His Holiness would be calling it 'avarice' and 'pride' if the message came from some other town! Were the Goths not heathens? Did Attila know anything of Christ or Our Lady? Have you not taught me that Rome fell before them both in the days of old?"

"Peace," answered the father. "There is nothing we can do but pray that this Admiral Balan is no Attila. And there are some things we might accomplish if the enemy spares us the time. Consider this..."

He went on to discuss his plans and ideas. By the time he'd finished Aimery had actually started to smile.

MEANWHILE, an argument raged in the Saracen camp over exactly that question: how to best use the next few days. On one side were the Admiral's Uncle Corsuble, his son Fierabras, and the brother Kings from Spain, Brullant and Clarion. Corsuble presented their case.

"Speed and daring have ever been the surest roads to victory in war. The Romans fought well today, but we won in the end. They fled because they had to. We should follow hard on their heels and attack before the city has a chance to prepare its defenses. A French army could arrive in as little as six or eight weeks if the Pope sends for aid. We should strike now, defeat the weaker foe before he has a chance to prepare, and then make ready for the one we need to fear."

King Iblis of Samarkand led the opposition, and answered this argument with scorn.

"*Fear?* Does a wolf fear the fragile doe? Exactly so much do I fear these French! To me they are prey and nothing more. I welcome their arrival!" He turned to face the Admiral. "Sire, if you will grant me the hand of thy daughter Floripas, I will swear here and now to bring thee the King of France and all his Twelve Peers – in irons or in coffins as they prefer. That is the measure of respect they deserve!"

This was no small request, for Floripas was no little prize. Any princess may be desired for that reason alone, but Floripas was extraordinary in her right too. Her waist was so tiny that a man might encircle it completely with his hands, her hair was like the richest gold, and here features were exceptional and fine; straight eyebrows, a slender nose, soft cheeks blushed with pink, a mouth that hinted of cherry and plum, and a high, generous curve to her proud bosom. Men said she was "bright as a rose in May" and it was true. She was, moreover, wise in the ways of herbs and magic, and the owner of a magic girdle that enhanced her beauty so much that a man who'd fasted for three or four days could be sated just by glimpsing her across the room.

Nevertheless, the Sultan liked those words right well. He embraced Iblis and said, "Let it be done. Floripas shall be yours."

The young lady rose to object. "Make no haste to deliver your gifts, Father. Samarkand shall have neither finger nor favor from me until I see these Frenchmen in chains with my own two eyes! Words and boasts count for nothing. Only deeds can be trusted. Besides, those are promises for the months ahead. Wasn't this meeting called to decide the fate of tomorrow?"

King Iblis waved this away. "There are other reasons to bide here a while. Even now our soldiers are descending from the sea. If we but wait to array our force together, the Romans shall be so struck with terror that they will surrender without any fight at all. We are also told that this land is rich in farms and vineyards. Grant me a week to forage about and I shall bring Your Majesty 10,000 virgins, twice as many barrels of wine, and enough victuals to supply our army until the French straggle their way down. Wine and women! What better way to ready an army for war?"

Fierabras uttered a snort of contempt, but then the Admiral's counselor King Sortibrant intervened to argue on Iblis' behalf. An hour later the Admiral had agreed. The Saracens would bide by the shore to mass their forces before attacking the city itself.

CHAPTER 2 – THE SARACEN ASSAULT

Eight days later, the Sultan summoned King Iblis and gave to him this command: "Tomorrow we attack. Look that you tarry no more! You shall lead the vanguard with thirty thousand of our finest Turks and Moors.

"Go to the city of Rome and beat down the gate; walls, towers and stones alike. The rest of the army shall march on your heels."

Iblis blew his horn to assemble the men and then rode off. No man can say he was pleased by what he found.

While the Saracens had been looting, Duke Hernaut had organized the Romans to dig a series of dikes around the city, which they joined to the river to create a moat that circled the entire wall. The water within was so devilishly deep, swift, and broad that the Saracens could not hope to swim across, and the river at either kept them from creeping around. They were like an army of ants trying to assault an island. Even boats would be useless, for the Romans had embedded so many spikes on the far side that it would be impossible for men to disembark.

Iblis took one look and then returned to the Sultan. "Your Majesty, our labors have all been in vain. The moat is so vast and well built that by Mahon I can not see how we should even reach their walls."

Admiral Balan waxed mightily wroth at these words. Tears poured from his eyes and foam from his lips in such great quantity that he could barely speak at all. No one dared to even approach him until his counselor Sortibrant plucked up enough courage to kneel before the throne.

"Do not lose hope Sire. A way will open if we trust in our gods. Make sacrifice to Mahon and Termagant to beg for their aid, and then send our engineers to review the Roman works. King Iblis is a mighty knight and the master of a vast nation, but his skills at siegecraft may yet be surpassed by those who know the trade better."

To this the Admiral agreed. Fifty captives went to the heathen altars, there to be strangled alive or to have their eyes torn out and their entrails used for prophesy and spells. Then Sir Corsuble, who knew all there was to know about war, rode out with the engineer Mavone to view the moat. Between them this pair had besieged and conquered more cities than most knights see in a lifetime. They rode the entire circuit before returning that evening to report to Admiral Balan.

THE MEETING took place in the Admiral's tent around a table large enough to hold twenty of the heathen war leaders and chiefs. "What say you, Uncle?" asked the Sultan. "Are the works as strong as men have said?"

"Strong, yes. But not invincible. We should have attacked right away. This is what comes from waiting. These new defenses will costs us two or three weeks of extra work."

"Weeks!" the Admiral exploded.

"It could be a month if they have a clever captain in charge of the defense." Corsuble spread a large sketch of the city on the table, and then explained its position above the river.

"Your Majesty will recall the intelligence we had before this invasion. Rome is built on a series of seven hills. The ancients protected the city with high walls, but also a set of gates to guard the approach. It begins with this road here." He drew a snaking line on the map, crossing back and forth in front of the city. "It is broad, well paved, and wide enough for all the farmers and merchants of Italy to climb their way up in days of peace. But climb they must, for it is an exceedingly long road and it only goes up. In truth, it is more like a gigantic ramp more than anything else, built so that defenders on the higher elevations can rain down arrows on those who move beneath."

The general paused to sketch in a wedge shape on the side to illustrate a piece of the road, then added dark lines on each side. "Nor is there any way for those so assailed to respond, for the hills on either side of the road have been cunningly carved into the sheerest of cliffs."

Corsuble added a thick, double line to the map, cutting across the center of the rising road. "Some hundred feet above the plain, after a quarter mile or so of road, we will encounter the first of the actual defenses: a gate built from entire trees, faced with steel, and set into a crenellated wall like the strongest of castles. The Romans claim this gate has stood untouched and unchallenged since the days of Attila."

Balan smiled wickedly. "Attila and engines are one thing. Astrogot and Mambrino are another. Continue."

King Corsuble gave a little bow and then said, "After the Forward Gate the road climbs on until it comes the walls of the town itself, some 300 feet above the river. The City Gate is only slightly less formidable than the first, being made of ancient oak seasoned to the hardness of stone. Beyond that there is a portcullis, and then the way is clear."

"This is what we knew before," said the Admiral. "Tell me now of this moat they've managed to raise."

Corsuble drew a half-ring around the city beginning and ending at the river to north and south. "At the northern point a sort of dam diverts the river's flow into this new channel. The ditch is no more than thirty feet wide and eight or ten feet deep, but that is enough to serve its purpose. It cannot be filled or forded, and it is protected against boats. It will have to be bridged instead, and that will take time. Once we are across, however, the moat will be as nothing." He pointed at the map and said, "All we'll need to do is destroy the dam. Do that and the water will drain of its own accord."

"Why not take it by storm?" King Iblis demanded from the other side of the table. "Weren't you the one talking about speed and daring just a few days hence? Why are you suddenly afraid to take chances?"

"There is a line between daring and foolish, Sir Iblis." The general glared at him. "Lives must be spent in war, just like coin. Wasting those lives is a sin."

King Sortibrant rose to support his friend. "Better a few lives than weeks of delay. Besides, these Christians are cowards to a man. Everyone knows that. I've little doubt that when they see our numbers, they will lay down their arms in surrender."

"Those were no cowards who fought us on the shore last week," Fierabras objected. "What you propose will be a slaughter. Our men will have to swim across the water unarmored, in easy range of every kind of missile from men on the city walls – men we cannot reach with arrows of our own. Not one in a hundred will make it across unharmed. And what of those who do? How should they defend themselves against a sally from the city by armored men and knights?"

"Enough!" said Admiral Balan. "We have the soldiers to spare. What we don't have is time. Iblis shall lead his assault tomorrow, and the glory of any success shall belong to him alone." He slammed down a hand so hard that the table cracked in two. Kings and captains alike staggered back in surprise.

"We will *not* be caught outside these walls to face an army of French! I do not care if it costs a hundred thousand men to breach this moat and tear down those walls. Blood is fine. Blood is good. I am in the mood for blood. Just see that the work is done!"

Neither the wily old Corsuble nor the noble Fierabras was happy with these orders, but their frustrations were nothing compared those suffered by Duke Hernaut on the other side of the city walls. Even the sight of so great an army had failed to stir either Senate or Church from their complacence. The Saracens had no actual need for haste because Charlemagne was not on his way to relieve the city. The French had no hint that their aid might be required.

NOT THAT the Romans needed French help against the assault they faced the next day. It began in the morning when King Iblis drove

40,000 of his personal slaves into the water with whips and barbs at their backs. Not a man among this force wore more than a tunic on his back, nor carried more of a weapon than a dagger or tool gripped between his teeth. Their task was to swim the moat and then dig away at the spears and fences set into the opposite side. With that done, Iblis planned to assault across the stream on makeshift rafts and boats.

Matters befell exactly as Fierabras and Corsuble had foreseen. Swimmers died by the tens of thousands under a storm of arrows and shot from the city walls. Each and every one of those archers had been practicing their range for more than a week. Misses were rare. By contrast, the enemy could not even return their fire because of the defenders' advantage in height. Duke Hernaut added another obstacle by raising the flow in the moat. Before long the stream looked like a river swollen with springtime rain. Even so the channel became so clogged with bodies that later waves could all but walk across.

Eventually of course, a few did make it to the other side, but it did them no good. Young Aimery rode forth with 10,000 spearmen, slew the survivors at will, and then tossed them back in the stream like so many unwanted fish. The slaughter went on until both the river to the sea beyond were filled with Saracen bodies. The Admiral lost 40,000 men in the attempt. The Romans lost two, plus another six with wounds that later healed.

At the end of the day both Aimery and his father were too tired and too sickened to even take joy in the triumph. They could only stare at the drifting dead and shake their heads in horror.

THREE DAYS later the water was clear. The next assault came under the command of King Corsuble, in the form of an armada sailing upstream from the ocean. The Admiral stood by the shore, watching at the side of his Uncle. "Will it work?" he asked the older man.

"There is a chance Your Majesty, but only if the defense is led by fools. Or priests. Or merchants, I suppose. Otherwise... Ah. See there."

He pointed as five great stones rose lazily up from the city and then plummeted down toward a carrick that led the Saracen fleet. Only one of the stones struck home; a glancing blow that sent the injured ship wallowing toward shore. The other craft immediately dropped their anchors just out of range.

"Will you not force the attack?" asked the Admiral.

"It would serve no purpose now that we know they are prepared."

"Then why bother?"

"Sitting where they are, those ships cost the Romans thirty thousand men. At the bottom of the river they'd help us not at all."

"NO YOUR HOLINESS," said Duke Hernaut, "we should *not* take heart from stopping the advance of their ships. Quite the opposite."

"I don't understand," said the Pope. "If our first defense was a triumph, why not this one as well?"

"The other day was a test of our resolve, no more, and whoever planned it was a fool. Today we saw a different mind, and a very dangerous one. Sailing the stream cost him nothing. But from this day on it costs us half our engines of defense, and all those needed to man them, simply to watch and make sure they stay where they are. They are stronger and we are weaker. And he's making sure that we know it."

"What will come next?" asked the Pope.

"Bridges," Hernaut replied. "Slow, steady, and inevitable. We'll make them pay for it, but they'll be across in a week once the things are built.

"Sir Pope, even King Charles will need some time to assemble enough strength to meet so great a host. Perhaps you should reconsider..."

The Pope held up a hand to forestall the plea. "The decision has been made. You may choose to see this day as a threat, but I see it as another victory. The Senate will do the same." He turned his back and walked away.

THE FIRST of the bridges arrived two days later, cunningly contrived to float upon the waters and yet be strong enough to bear the weight of assaulting troops. Engineer Mavone seemed like a proud father as he presented it to the Admiral and King Corsuble.

"It will hold twelve men across," he explained, "or four armored knights in a file. And we've built it in pieces that may be erected wherever you wish, Majesty. The Christians may see us coming, but they cannot know where we will try to cross until the work begins tomorrow morning. And doubt it not: within an hour from when we start the bridge will be ready to use. Isn't she lovely?"

"Quite," said Corsuble, and then ushered the man out of the way. "I want to warn you nephew: the bridge will go up, I have no doubt, but tomorrow will be a bloody day. When all is said and done just a few of ours may cross at a time, and the Romans shall array themselves on the other side – the barest fingertip of our strength against the entire hand and arm of the city. But eventually, I deem, our numbers will tell. The next bridge is already being built, and Mavone will start on a third one tomorrow."

The Admiral narrowed his eyes with anger. "I find your lack of faith disturbing, Uncle. They may be waiting when we try to cross, but they cannot be ready for what we will be sending!"

The ancient general shrugged. "In war it is always better to prepare for the worst. We hope to surprise them on the morrow. This Duke who leads them is shrewd enough to plan some surprises of his own. I've done this long enough to know. The first day is always the worst."

EVEN AS the pair retired, on the other side of the stream Duke Hernaut was speaking to the assembled captains of Rome.

"I do not trust this new general of theirs. Mark my words – he won't just march his men across that bridge and into a pocket of steel. He's prepared some kind of trick, and we will be lost if we don't do the same."

"What do you think he has planned?" asked Aimery.

"I haven't a clue," said his father. "That's what worries me. But we've got to be ready for whatever it is." They stayed up late into the night imagining possibilities and devising ways to respond.

THE BRIDGE came together the next morning despite all the Christians did to oppose it. Arrows, shot and trebuchet stones alike; all had been foreseen by the Saracens' master engineer and the lore of their general. But that is not to say the Romans were unprepared.

Duke Hernaut arrayed his forces around the bridgehead in such a way that any man who dared set foot on the Roman side would be facing a wall of shields and spears from all directions. Stakes had been planted in haste to prevent a charge by even the heaviest of armored knights. Obstacles of all variety were scattered about as well, to guard against everything the defenders had been able to imagine, from chariots like those of ancient Troy to armored wagons or rams that might be used to break the Christian lines.

What came instead were giants: two giants, each one half again the size of Fierabras and armed in a manner that set the stoutest of hearts atremble with fear.

Astrogot the Moor came first, dressed in armor formed from steel plates as thick as a normal man's thumb, and so heavy that the bridge sagged under his weight alone. As if that wasn't enough, he held a shield that was eight feet across in one hand, and a man-sized iron mace in the other, shaped at the top like the head of a full-grown boar. The weapon alone weighed more than most horses, but Astrogot swung it with no more effort than a normal man would need for a slender sword.

For those with the wit to consider the matter, Astrogot's brother King Mambrino stirred an even deeper fear. This was because he wore... nothing. Where Astrogot had plate to cover his body, Mambrino had naught but trews on his legs and a flapping tunic on his slate-gray arms. The only thing that remotely looked like a tool of war sat on his head: a golden helmet, smooth and unadorned. But that was enough and more than enough, for the helm contained a virtue that protected its wearer from harm of any kind. The keenest sword caused no more hurt than a tiny kitten's claw, nor the sharpest spear more than a budding thorn. Mambrino bore no shield because he had no need, and he bore no weapon because he disdained their use. Instead he would pick up his foes like meat from a table and smash them down to the ground, leaving only broken forms in his wake.

Behind these monsters came an endless trickle of footmen, twelve abreast across the bridge and bearing heavy shields to ward off shot from all directions. Fierabras himself waited on shore to exploit any weakness. King Brullant sat ready on his right, King Clarion to his left, and King Iblis to his rear with 50,000 Turks trained to war since the day they were born.

Duke Hernaut and his 10,000 Romans could in no way prevent the giants from crossing the bridge. They had no means to cause the monsters harm, and precious few men had the courage to even approach Astrogot and his fearsome club. The Romans could, however, hold the pair at bay like a pack of miniature hounds harassing the great brown bear.

Behind and around the giants was another matter. The Saracen foot soon realized that naught but death could be found by delaying near their bridge. "Forward!" came the word from their officers in the rear. "Follow the giants through their lines!"

This proved to be little better. The giants could open a path, no doubt, but they could not help to maintain it. Whenever they stood in one place, Romans darted forward with entangling nets and ropes that threatened to pin them down despite their strength. This strategy forced the pair to rampage off time and again, leaving the infantry isolated, unsupported, and lacking any path toward their only line of escape.

The Christian knights fell on these concentrations like lightning on a drought-dry field, and the Saracens simply could not amass enough men to resist a mounted charge. Their formations crumbled into panic, at which point the men themselves were quickly slain or driven to drown in the moat.

The battle pulsed throughout the day, long and savage, but at the end things remained much as they'd been at the start. The defenders retired to their walls with only a few score lost, mostly to the giants, while the pagans left so many dead that their bodies made all but another wall.

The Admiral waxed wild with rage but Corsuble reassured him. "We knew there would be blood, Sire. Did I not say that the first assault is always the worst? Today we have taken their measure. Tomorrow it will be a closer thing, and the days after that better still. Our strength is endless. Rome's is not. And soon there will be a second bridge at the other side of the city. Then a third, and if needs be a fourth and a fifth. 'Tis simply a matter of time."

ALAS FOR ROME, but this Saracen knew his craft well. The next day's assault was again led by the invincible giants, this time supported by men whose sole task was to keep them free of entangling nets and the like. It limited the damage that either giant could do, but at the same time it allowed the rest of the army to slowly advance in their wake. The valiant Duke and his men imposed on the foe a heavy price, but at sunset the Saracens held both sides of their bridge.

By the end of the third day a few of the enemy's knights were able to cross as well. The defenders could only watch as Fierabras himself led the slow trickle of pagan banners, followed close behind by the warrior kings Brullant and Clarion.

Duke Hernaut spoke to his force as the enemy began to form up for a charge: "Now come the days of peril! Only the sturdiest hearts can hope to save our homes! You must understand what we face: Here by the shore we have many to match their few. But if we leave this bridge unguarded a flood will begin that no man could staunch.

"The enemy will attack in a moment. Some will break out from our cordon. It is inevitable. Your task shall be a hard one. You must – must! – ignore the enemy at your back and maintain your watch here. If a dozen of their knights should ride toward the city, you must trust that I will be there with a thousand of ours to track them down. No matter the temptation, you *must* bide here and keep the mass contained."

Fists banged against chests in the ancient Roman salute. "It shall be as you command, Your Grace!" A storm of cheers arose to follow that declaration.

Duke Hernaut was a knight of ancient blood and well earned fame. There was no more valorous man to be found in all of Christendom save the Paladins who served King Charles, and he would have fit at their table. Indeed, his brother and his nephew sat close to its head. No man in all of Christendom stood higher in blood, or valor, or accomplishment than this worthiest of heroes.

But the enemy had mighty champions of its own, as events soon proved.

The Saracens charged not a minute later and nothing the Romans did could contain them. The iron club of Astrogot cleared a path; the invulnerable Mambrino marched through it, snatching grown men from their steeds as if they were children; and then came Fierabras, all in black save the glittering jewels on his helm, slaying wherever he went. Duke Hernaut had spoken of a dozen men marauding across the field. By noon that had swelled to a thousand, and he was forced the one extremity he'd sworn to avoid until the end was nigh – drawing strength from those by the bridge. The end was drawing close, and both sides knew it.

Then trumpets sounded from the city walls and the gates opened for a charge of 25,000 militia led by the Pope himself.

Now it was the heathen knights who found themselves sore pressed, and in imminent danger of losing their only path to safety. King Iblis led the retreat at one part of the field. For all his pride it must be said that the heathen king was a fearsome man of war. Eighteen Romans he slew by himself in his fight to gain the bridge, including a Senator named Guicharde who had slain ten Saracen knights before riding against this one. Iblis struck him from the saddle almost without thought, along with three worthy squires who rode by his side.

Fierabras led on the other side, sounding a call on his silver horn and then struggling to carve his own way out. The first unfortunate who barred his path was a man in in rich clothing named Sir Briere of Poyle. The Roman fell in a moment, pierced through with a spear and dead before he hit the ground. Sir Giacomo, another worthy man, rode full upon the Admiral's son to avenge his fallen friend. Fierabras didn't even see him coming. Only the rumbling rise of hooves and the instinct of a life at war allowed the Saracen prince to slide his enormous shield in the way.

Giacomo's lance shattered at the impact, but delivered its force nonetheless. Fierabras fell into a trance from the shock alone, and his charger buckled at the knees. Sir Giacomo drew his sword and closed in to seize the advantage. The first blow cut off a shower of gems from Fierabras' glittering helm. The second fell heavy upon his shoulder, but could not pierce the coat of gilded plates. Many more good strokes followed apace and Fierabras was sore aggrieved. Indeed he might have fallen if King Brullant had not intervened.

The Spanish king slammed his stallion into the side of Sir Giacomo's mount, and then followed with a blow from his mace that sent the Christian stumbling away in a daze of his own. Brullant didn't pursue. Instead he laughed aloud with the joy of battle and pointed his mace at Fierabras. "Stop playing with your food!" he called. "We've a full feast laid on the table and little time to dally!"

Then he laughed again and rode off to fight his way toward the bridge.

Sir Giacomo set spurs to his mount and charged once again at Fierabras. This time, however, the giant was ready. Even worse, he'd found a chance to draw his sword. A single, mighty stroke from Plourance cut through the Roman's neck; aventail, gorget, and all. The stroke was so swift and clean that Giacomo's mount continued on to the end of the field bearing a headless rider like some ghost from a fireside tale.

Fierabras watched him go and then stood in his stirrups to examine the field. The Pope himself stood on a low hill but a small distance away: mounted, in full armor, and riding beneath a high banner that flapped in the breeze. A feral smile lit the Saracen's lips. "This must be the sovereign of Rome!"

He urged his steed to a charge, cut through the guards, and in the space of moments bore the Pope down from his mount and onto the grassy field. Leaping from the saddle, Fierabras ripped off his opponent's helm – only to discover the shaven pate of a monk. The sight filled him with shame.

"Fie, priest, God give thee sorrow! What are you doing, armed in the field, when you should be saying your prayers instead? I hoped to have felled an Emperor. A chieftain of the host. Someone worthy of conquest! Instead I have... you." He shook his head in disgust.

"Go home to your choir! Giving you the death you've earned would shame me for certain."

The Pope was glad of this speech, you may be sure. He certainly did naught but obey.

So the battle continued, hard and strong until the heathen had finally given over completely. Many a steed went astray or lay wounded on the ground to never rise again. Nine hundred of the pagans' pride were slain that day in the field, plus thousands who'd fought afoot . Eight hundred Romans lost arms, or legs, or lives. More than their share were noteworthy men, for the Saracens took special care to target any man whose array bespoke a position of leadership.

The Roman day had ended in triumph. The danger was averted, the enemy driven back, and their works cut loose to float downstream.

The news was all good. The tidings were not.

The floating bridge had suffered great harm, but a few days labor would see it fully repaired. By then the second bridge would be ready and the third well underway. The Romans had won a lull in the storm, but all could see that the clouds were closing in.

Messengers departed for France that night; three separate men in three separate directions, each bearing a copy of the city's cry for help. Duke Hernaut's son Sir Aimery was given the most direct and dangerous of the paths. But France was a long way distant and all men knew that the plea had been sent too late.

CHAPTER 3 – THE SIEGE OF ROME

The Saracen mood that night was no more happy than the one in the city. The Admiral of Spain was never known for his patience. The morning had savored of victory. The city's charge had turned that taste to ashes. Now Balan's rage was terrible to behold. His rampage through the camp slew a dozen men that chanced to be in his way.

Even his closest advisor, Sortibrant, did not dare to approach him. He and King Iblis could only follow their lord around and call out the occasional warning. The storm went on until the sun dipped low and the lovely Floripas intervened.

"This is absurd," she said. "It is nigh on the hour for dinner and I, for one, am hungry. If you do not know how to handle such a mood I advise you to watch and learn!"

She had a single low bench placed in the Admiral's path and then arrayed herself to wait. As he thundered her way she contrived a flood of tears so that when he came near, her cheeks were swollen and soaked, her hair disheveled, and her delicate chin quivering in a display of abject desolation.

"I cannot stand it!" she moaned. "I cannot! It isn't fair!" She rocked in the seat, twisting at her skirts with delicate little fists.

Seeing her thus brought the Admiral to a halt. "Daughter? What is it? What is wrong?"

She shook her head and turned away. Grief had clearly overwhelmed her ability to speak. He sat on the bench beside her and reached around her shoulders in an awkward attempt at comfort. After a long moment she seemed to melt, and laid her head against his chest.

"There now," he said. "Enough with the tears. Tell me what is wrong."

"I hate this place," she said at last, with a sniffle against his shirt. "I am sick and tired of tents! I want to stay in a proper room – in Rome! – with proper walls and a roof that won't heave in the wind. I want to wear shoes that aren't all muddy! And I'm hungry," she said.

"If Rome you want, then Rome you shall have. A week will see us against the walls, I deem. After that we will find a way. But a meal we can get right now. No wonder you're hungry. Look, it's dinner time!"

He raised her up, put her hand inside his arm, and gently escorted her toward the waiting smell of meat. King Sortibrant turned to Iblis who stood beside him.

"Men wield swords and we call them strong. Women wield men and we call them weak. Explain this to me."

"That is my promised bride," said Iblis, "and I mean to have her. Remember this Sortibrant. Remember and never forget: Women are changeable, inconstant, and not to be trusted. Just think of how many men have been led astray by the doings of women! One simply has to be firm."

Sortibrant nodded. "You are a wise man, Iblis. Your suit shall have my fullest support."

THE SARACENS prepared their assault with exceeding care as the last of the floating bridges neared completion. Corsuble, Fierabras and Brullant made careful arrangements for every detail they could imagine, from who should cross at which particular spot to what they should do when they had. But it was King Iblis who contrived the most devious and devilish of all the heathen plots.

"We know how this day will go at the end," he told the assembled commanders. "We shall erect our bridges. Duke Hernaut will come out to challenge our crossing. Many a bout and battle shall ensue, for he is a brave and worthy man. But in the end he will be forced to retire because his numbers are too few to defend at so many locations. At that point our forces will destroy the Christians' dam by the river, the moat will empty, and our army will face naught but a soggy ditch until we reach the Forward Gate."

"This is the plan," King Corsuble agreed.

"You must think further, old man!" said Iblis. "What will Hernaut do when he realizes the day is lost?"

"Retire up the road and defend the gate."

"Exactly! And what would happen if his way was barred?"

"He and his men would be utterly destroyed. But we have discussed this," said Corsuble. "Until we take the riverside fort we won't have enough men to keep the Romans away from their gate. Any force we might dispatch would be attacked from all directions: by darts from the walls, by men from the city, and by Hernaut himself striving to return."

"True enough. But what if the gate itself was destroyed, even for just a moment?" Iblis laughed. "We could wring their necks like so many chickens in the yard while the Romans watched from their walls."

"And you have a plan to accomplish this?"

"I do," said Iblis. "I do indeed."

TO NO ONE'S surprise the day began exactly as the generals on both sides had foreseen. The Romans had devised certain clever devices that delayed the assault in one location. By dint of sheer courage and daring, Duke Hernaut enforced a heavy toll on the Saracens at their other crossings too. But cross they did. The Christians simply could not defend three separate breaches in their wall of water.

By noon Fierabras himself was free in the field with 5,000 fearsome Turks at his side. Many sharp battles took place then, with many a shock and surprise. The air grew heavy with the sounds and scents of war and death. But all men knew how it was bound to end. Moment by moment the Saracen strength increased while the defenders were left on their own.

At this point Iblis put his plan into action. During the many weeks they'd been checked the Saracens had come to know Duke Hernaut's banners and attire as well as they knew their own. Iblis had an identical set created, down to the colors and barding worn by the mounted men who accompanied the Duke most often.

Now, with the battle waxing fierce and the true Duke hidden in the fray, Iblis hurried up the ramp with a hundred men dressed in this disguise and waving his counterfeit flag.

"Open the gate!" he cried. "Clear a path for the Duke!"

Supposing Iblis to be Hernaut, the Romans opened the way to this false contrivance and thus lost more – far more – than just a line of defense. The Saracens slew all within and took control of the Forward Gate. Then they commenced to wait. They did not open it. Oh no. That might have been seen in the city. They barred the doors shut and jammed the works.

OUT ON the field of battle, the real Duke Hernaut led his men against ever more desperate odds, judging to the finest nuance how long it might take to break away when the day was finally lost. There was no chance whatsoever to hold the field. Victory today would be counted in the number of lives it cost the enemy to take it.

Close on noon a Saracen cheer went up by the river.

"My lord, what has happened?" asked one of the younger knights.

"The riverside fort has fallen, and with it the dam and works that let us maintain our moat. A candlemark, two at the most, and their way will be clear. Sound your horns!" he cried. "The hour has come to fall back on the city!"

The signal echoed forth across the field. A fighting retreat can be hard to manage but in this case every Roman man had been warned the moment would come. All had been carefully prepared. Even the inter-ference of the Admiral's giants had been planned for, as had the inevitable charges from Fierabras and his men, who – for the moment – lacked enough numbers to restrain the Roman defenders. There were no surprises until the retreating men came to their own doors and found the way barred against them.

"Open!" yelled Hernaut. "Open I say! There are thirty thousand of your brothers and sons who seek the safety of their homes!"

The massive, steel-faced passage stayed shut.

"Open!" the Duke said again. "This is no time for a jest!"

The answer came with a laugh that held no humor. "Jest?" called King Iblis. "Who has need of jests? The destruction of my enemies is all the amusement I require!"

The Christian army had nothing that even resembled the equipment needed to besiege so great a tower as the Forward Gate of Rome. Why would knights ride to battle with ladders? All they could was return to the fray and extract as heavy a price as they could for their lives. Many great deeds were undoubtedly done and many a stand that was worthy of song. None can be related for no one lived with a heart to tell the tale. Rhyme if you would of thirty thousand souls who rode off in the morn, and returned as sixty and two. That was the sum of those who survived to be captured.

SUCH A LOSS was dear enough, but the Pope knew well it was worse than the numbers alone. The cream of Roman chivalry had been destroyed, and that was a terrible stroke. Duke Hernaut was dead, who could not be replaced. That was even worse. But worst of all, the city had lost both its outer moat and its Forward Gate in the space of a morning. Nothing remained but the city wall itself.

The pontiff sent men throughout the town to summon the populace for a great service to be held at Saint Peter's. There he displayed the high banner of Rome and absolved every man from the judgment of God. Then he prayed to Saint Peter and to Paul for help and succor, and also to Our Lady, that sweet flower, to save the city of Rome from woe.

Then the Pope went outside, where he gave a funeral mass for the fallen and preached courage to those who survived.

"Our walls are high and thick. If our hearts stay true, then God will support us through this peril until King Charles of France can arrive to break the siege. Word was dispatched before this latest disaster. By now Our messengers are nigh on the King himself. When He arrives with all his famous knights – Roland, Oliver, Ogier, and the rest – the heathen shall pay in full measure for all the destruction he has wrought!"

A sigh of relief went through the crowd at the mention of Charlemagne. The names of his paladins brought an actual cheer. In peacetime, many had doubted the fanciful tales men told of their prowess. Now fear and hope conjoined to remove all questions. The people of this Rome looked toward the coming of Roland even as their forefathers must have looked toward the coming of Caesar on his three-toed horse, or Alexander the Great on his splendid Bucephalus.

THE SARACENS attacked the city at sunrise. By land the Admiral ordered his men forward with ladders, pikes, and bills to overthrow the walls and slay the Romans within. By water he ordered boats sent in with sailors to fight hand to hand on the docks. And on every side he erected mighty trebuchets strong enough to span the city walls with boulders to break the buildings within. The enemy host pressed in against every corner and from all directions.

Highborn and low alike joined the defense with equal desperation. Men ran to the towers that were in the greatest doubt, where many sharp battles ensued. Wives and maidens bore stones to the walls as fast as they could, trembling with dread and care. The defenders cast them over the walls. Ten thousand Saracens and more were killed on the first day alone. But their numbers were endless.

As the third day dawned the Saracens waxed mightily proud. Admiral Balan called up to the Romans.

"Yield now, for you may not long endure! Yield and I will spare your lives! Resist and I swear by Mahon that all shall be slain!"

A Roman then loosed a dart that smote him though the breastplate, but not the hauberk beneath. The Sultan went more than mad with fury at this effrontery. He cried to Fierabras, "For Mahon's love destroy both man and place! Spare nothing that is alive or standing – neither house, tower, nor wall; beast, servant, nor man; child, woman, nor dog in the street. Burn, slay and destroy it all!"

Fierabras immediately called for both Sortibrant and the engineer Mavone. "Are your engines good? Show me now your craft! Let the sky be filled with shot and stone to beat down both tower and wall. If a building still stands when the day is done I shall account your work as a failure."

But for all the rocks and shot that flew threw the air, the greatest danger lay at the gate. There the assault was led by the wily Corsuble, ably assisted by the invulnerable giant Mambrino and his monstrous brother Astrogot, who was just as large and twice as strong. First the general commanded that endless thousands of Saracen archers should fill the air with shot and dart so that any Roman who dared to even approach these wards would be sure to perish. Then the giants, defiant of the men who dared the walls nonetheless, marched toward the gate.

"May Termagant blast me and Apollo burn me to a cinder if I return tonight with this door unbroken!" said Astrogot.

Full sorry were the Romans when he proved to be as good as his boast. The Forward Gate had been faced with steel. The City Gate was made of wood alone. It was good wood; thick, strong, and well cared for. But no tree in all of Europe could have hoped to withstand the Iron Mace of Astrogot.

Once he struck, and the boom echoed so loudly that Romans looked up in fear, wondering at the marvel of thunder in a clear blue sky. Twice he struck, and the doors shivered in their frame. A third time he struck, and cracks appeared from top to bottom.

The giant laughed in triumph, reached back with all his might, and drove his mighty club against the doors for the fourth and final time. The Gate of Rome shattered beneath his stroke like an old clay pot assailed by the blacksmith's sledge.

A score of soldiers had been waiting behind the gate to face whatever fate God should choose to deliver. When they saw that fate step forward, all covered in armor and bearing a mace bigger than any of the men himself, their courage seemed to fly as quickly as the door. As a single man with forty legs the Romans fled up the tunnel toward the city.

The sound of their shrieks and the sight of their backs was all it took to spur the giant forward. Astrogot pursued with a roar of triumph. But alas for him, the Roman retreat had in truth been a ruse.

Even as the monster ran forward, the guards within let fall their final defense: a portcullis of heavy steel with blades at the bottom sharpened like the finest spear. The crashing points smote Astrogot through and through: heart, liver and gall alike. He lay crying on the ground so loud that the sound went through the city like a Devil's horn.

Glad indeed were the Romans to see this fearsome brute slain in their trap. And sorry indeed were the Saracens when they heard of his ill-fated charge.

The Sultan, Fierabras, and Iblis as well withdrew to their tents in mourning, leaving the giant's corpse where it lay. The assault ended for the day.

'TWOULD BE wrong to say the Saracens were celebrating in their camp that evening. Astrogot had been mighty among the heathen kings, and loved more than most besides. Even the Admiral sorrowed at his death. But neither were they frustrated with the progress of their siege.

"Now that the gate is down it will be but a matter of time," said Corsuble. "Days if Your Majesty repeats his generous terms. A few weeks if the populace know they face destruction. A month at the most will see the city's fall."

"A month!" protested King Iblis. "Who knows where Charlemagne may be if we wait a full month? I have a better way."

The Sultan greeted this with interest but also a fair amount of skepticism.

"You, Sir Iblis, boasted to conquer the Romans and to bring me in chains all Twelve Peers and Charlemagne their king. Upon that condition I granted you my daughter, Dame Floripas. Do you now seek to change your offer?"

"So I said," Iblis granted, "and so I shall do. Yea, all that and more will I do for the sake of Floripas' hand. I do not seek to avoid our bargain. Far from it! What I propose is a better means to achieve it.

"We must take the city as soon as may be, so that a trap may be set for the French when they come to relieve it. Wherefore I ask that you allow me to uphold my part of the covenant in such manner as I deem best.

"I also say this: your Uncle, King Corsuble, would offer terms to the city as a means to speed their surrender. Who can doubt that some of those who accept your terms will straightaway abandon their oaths and fly to the French with warning? My way requires only a single pardon – for I have a traitor within the walls. The rest of the city may then be put to the sword, or sold into slavery as Your Majesty may wish."

"What are the traitor's terms?" asked the Sultan.

"Hear his words for yourself and then judge if they should be accepted."

The traitor's name was Lubys, a Christian knight from the east. He had come to Rome seeking the favor of the Pope, and had prospered when he found it. Like many of his sort this Lubys possessed a high position within the city but little in the way of respect from those who actually knew him. Though named a knight, he was in fact a coward who had feigned injury during the battles outside the wall and then dipped his sword in the blood of the dead to hide his disgrace.

The Pope and Senators thought him clever and sage. Most recently it was Lubys who had thought to use the women of the town to aid in its defense. What they'd failed to realize was this: the odious man had suggested the idea in order to take himself down into safety in the guise of "organizing" those selfsame women and children. When they went forward to fight he stayed in their places of shelter to "look for more who should help the defense." Thus was the character of Lubys, who now presented his plan to the Admiral of Spain.

"My lord, I have in my house the widow of a man who died at the side of Duke Hernaut. Her husband was the chief porter of the town. This lady now holds his keys. If you will give grace for both my goods and for me, and grant me rule of these lands in Your name, I will take hold of those keys and deliver to you the city."

"Let it be so," said Balan. "You shall never know want again. Bread from my table shall be yours to the end of your days."

AS IT HAPPENED, young Sir Aimery was kneeling before Charlemagne at the very moment that Lubys was bending his knee to the heathen Admiral of Spain. The letters he bore had been received with grace, and read with growing concern. Now Aimery himself was there to report what he'd seen with his own two eyes.

"Sire, the enemy has not been kind in his occupation. Many tens of thousands have been slain out of hand, or sold into evil bondage across the sea. The country is burnt unto the gate of Rome itself. People and Pope alike sigh in despair and pray for succor from the arm of France."

"The Admiral of Spain?" said the King. "I count him as nothing. No man of mine shall rest until he and all his ilk have been ousted from Christendom."

He summoned Guy of Burgundy to his side, the King's nephew and a younger cousin of Roland.

"Guy, you are a knight who is good and true. Take our guard from here at Aix and a thousand pounds of gold as well. Head toward Rome at once, building your force as you go. Take care to move as fast as you can, for I feel in my gut that they have great need. The worst of this news is that it took so long to reach Us.

"Spare neither horse nor man but those who fall dead on the march. Duke Richard of Normandy is here at Court, as are William the Scot and Duke Thierry of Ardennes. They and their households shall ride at your side. I shall follow as soon as may be."

TWO DAYS of valorous defense passed in the city of Rome after the Sultan struck his bargain with Lubys. The third day proved to be different. It began in the dim hours just before dawn. Just a few miles away the gentle sky wept dew on sleepy leaves in a peaceful wood. In the city, however, Fierabras and twenty thousand chosen men stood by the great portcullis, waiting for the traitor to do his work.

As promised, the iron bars slowly rose. The Saracens moved with a silent, cat's paw tread into a still and empty square where Lubys stood by the device that controlled the final defense. The rest of the guard had been poisoned. Fierabras waved at his men to spread out into the city, and then strode to the traitor's side. He drove a great spike into the works, so that no man under heaven could close the way again.

Then he turned and smote off the traitor's head. It fell to the ground still smug and smiling.

"God forbid that the table where I eat should ever hold bread for a rascal like this! Thus must all traitors fare. If he would betray those here who'd raised him to positions of honor, he would betray me too if the chance arose. A traitor once is a traitor forever, and a poisoner is just as bad."

The heathens placed Lubys' head on a spear and carried it through the fair city, crying "Treason! Treason!"

What happened then was a pity to see. The people fled by every way, desperate for somewhere safe to abide. No such place existed. By noon the highways were full of dead men, and so was the side of every lane. Saracens spread from house to house faster and more deadly than any blaze.

Fierabras went straight to the Vatican Castle in search of the holy relics. The Pope himself charged at the giant knight with a spear. Fierabras brushed the weapon aside and seized the man by his throat.

"I know you, Priest. You're that fool I met on the field! I told you there to stay in your church and bend your hands to the reading of prayers. You should have listened."

So saying he struck off the Pontiff's head with the selfsame sword that had slain the traitor Lubys. The Cross, the Crown, and the bent Nails he took into his personal care. Then, having no taste for what he knew would follow, Fierabras returned to the gate and made way for Iblis and the Admiral. The Saracens took three days to sack the city and despoil it of treasure and gold. The people they took away as slaves, and then burnt all that remained.

A valiant defense takes many a song to explain. The sadder tale that follows calls for none.

CHAPTER 4 – A LADY'S FAVOR

The Admiral idled in Rome for a time to count his treasures before sending the loot by ship to his city of Aygremore in Spain. During that time King Iblis came into the Saracen Court.

"Sir Sultan, have I not given Rome unto your hand even as I promised?"

The Admiral allowed that he had. "But that was not our bargain. My daughter is promised, but she will remain unclaimed until you have given me Charlemagne and his Peers as well. In chains or in coffins, either will suffice. How do you plan to accomplish this?"

"We have learned that messengers were but lately sent to France," said Iblis. "None can doubt that the King will march for Rome as soon may be. But if he has even a hint of our numbers, and our prisoners have said that he does, even Charlemagne will need a space of many weeks to gather his vassals.

"Ask yourself this: What will he do in the meantime? Nothing, for a city he believes is still struggling to resist? Impossible! There is only one answer: the dotard of France shall dispatch whatever force he has to hand with orders to either save the city, or report on its fall and the state of our army. Five thousand men. Perhaps ten at most."

Iblis continued after the Admiral had nodded his understanding. "Now who will he send to lead this force? They must be men he trusts. And men of sufficient rank and reputation to impress the Romans. Who would such men be but Paladins? I cannot divine their particular names. Perhaps Duke Naymon, or Thierry. Perhaps Roland himself. The names I do not know. But their nature I can read as plain as the stars. In a month's time, no more, at least three of the Twelve Peers shall bring themselves here to our hands."

Several of the Admiral's council raised their voices in praise of Iblis' shrewd calculation. King Sortibrant spoke first.

"Doubt it not Sire. King Iblis has seen deep into the mind of our foe."

"Indeed," said Corsuble with grudging admiration. "I see no way in which he might have erred. 'Twould be a shame to have such guests arrive without a dance planned to receive them."

"My thinking exactly!" said Iblis. "Sir King, what I propose is this. Leave me here with 70,000 of our Arabs, Turks, and Abyssinians. We shall conceal them within the city and make it seem as if your siege has been lifted. The paladins may be suspicious but what can they do? Are they not tasked to report the truth of what they see? Will they not desire to take mass with their Pope? They will have but one choice, and that is to enter the walls to see the town for themselves.

"The moment they do we shall have them! All I ask is that you leave Floripas here as well. A bride should see the exploits of her husband to be."

The Admiral agreed to all of King Iblis' terms, adding only that Corsuble should remain as well to chaperone the maiden and assist with matters of war.

Balan and Fierabras set sail for Aygremore in another week's time to fill their days with mirth and joy. To their gods they made rich offerings of thanks. Before golden idols they burnt frankincense in such amounts that the fume of the first day's rite still lingered when the harvest was done. They blew horns of brass. They drank beast's blood. Milk and honey too, royal and good. Serpents were fried in oil and served on plates of Roman gold. *"Antrarian, antrarian"* they cried, meaning 'Joy for all.' Thus they lived in bliss.

But let us now be done with this, and speak of Sir Guy instead.

GUY OF NORMANDY, the nephew of Charlemagne, sped toward Rome with his host just as the King had commanded. Smoke from the burning city tainted the air even from a full day's march away. The land seemed utterly empty.

"Not a duck, or a dog, or a cow to be seen," said Duke Thierry. "'Tis an ill omen if ever I saw one."

But the city itself seemed different when they arrived. There were no flames, just the normal smoke to be expected of such a place. No cry of anger nor upset could be heard upon the air. All was quiet. Indeed, there was no movement at all save a few souls walking about on the city walls who seemed oblivious to everything else.

Duke Richard of Normandy, as wise in the ways of war as any save the King himself or perhaps the wise Duke Naymon, gestured toward the empty road that rose majestically up from the plain.

"Do not be deceived, Guy. If the city was at peace there would be merchants and the like moving to and fro. Farmers with wagons. Traders with goods. But if the city was destroyed there would be scavengers; birds and beasts, or worse. This... This makes no sense. I cannot imagine what would cause a city like Rome to assume so strange a pose, but I like it not."

"What would you counsel, Your Grace? We cannot just turn back to report so great a mystery to the King. We must know more."

Duke Richard nodded slowly. "I agree. You and I shall lead a party. Fifty men, no more. We must at least explore closer and speak to those people on the walls."

FLORIPAS watched the knights' cautious approach from where she perched on the ramparts. Her new maid stood beside her – a Roman woman named Maragonde who had converted to the worship of Mahon after the fall of the city. Floripas had taken the girl into service upon learning that she had waited on guests of the Pope himself, and knew both Charlemagne and many of his lords by sight.

The pair had enjoyed plenty of time to discuss those knights. Far too much time as Floripas saw it, for they'd been bound in her chambers for the better part of a month.

"It is Iblis' fault," she complained to her new maid. "He wants me close enough to see his prowess, but locked away at all other times like some jewel to be hidden from potential thieves. Uncle Corsuble is no better, but at least he bothers to explain himself."

In point of fact, Corsuble could not have been clearer. Within an hour of her father's departure the old man had drawn her aside, barking a laugh when she appeared with a display of maidenly airs and shyness.

"Bat your eyes all you like, Floripas. I know better. I've been on to you and your games since you sat on my knee as a little girl and complained that your needles were too short to be used as weapons. You have a will to match any Emperor or King.

"I know this too: You have set that will against your father's promise that the King of Samarkand may take you to wife. Do not bother to deny it! I have not come to alter your mind. You will do as you want, just as you always have. I come for a different reason."

She'd cast her eyes down in the most modest of ways, twining the silk about her fingers. "I cannot imagine what you mean, Uncle."

He'd snorted. "I'm fond of you, girl. Fond and proud, of you and your brother alike. But your father is my liege and I am a knight. Duty will always come first. Remember that. Don't let your battle against father and fiancé interfere with the duties that I am here to perform."

Seeing no adequate way to respond she had answered with silence. The result had been many weary days encased in her rooms with a flock of older women. She'd barely had a chance to see the city at all! Only recently had she devised a stratagem to at least get her out to the city walls. She'd broached the idea to Iblis over a meal, deeming him an easier target than her Uncle.

"You seek to create a semblance of normal life? How can you do that with no traffic into or out of the city? And no movement on the boulevards? The more my maid and I are seen on the walls, the more normal the place will seem."

This argument had won her a space of freedom. How she should use it remained to be seen.

GUY OF NORMANDY led the way toward the too-quiet city under a pall of heavy, gray clouds. A distinct whiff of smoke and death underlay the odor of well-churned mud. Barely a hint of grass had begun to reassert itself from the beaten ground. His charger, a young stallion, whickered nervously.

The sun broke through when the troop was no more than a hundred yards from the wall: a thin, brilliant beam that shone full on the young paladin in his gleaming plate and mail. The charger shied, rearing into the air and pawing at invisible foes. Guy brought the horse quickly under control. Style mattered when you were riding next to Richard of Normandy, the greatest horseman in Charlemagne's court.

It mattered in other ways too, though he could not know it at the time.

UP ON THE city wall Floripas regarded the prancing figure, her eyes aglow with wonder. "Who is that marvelous knight?" she asked her maid.

Maragonde peered over the wall and said, "I recognize him! That is Guy of Normandy. He sat at the King's table when I saw them two years ago. A nephew, I believe. Men say he's now one of the Twelve Peers though he wasn't back then."

"He's beautiful!" sighed Floripas. "Hello!" she called, waving a fine silk scarf that she'd embroidered during the weeks she'd been trapped inside. "Hello, Sir Knight!"

He looked up and her heart took flight like a sparrow launched from its nest. With an elegant gesture she tossed the filmy thing out upon the wind.

Down below the young horseman spurred his mount to a gallop, leaned to one side, and gracefully plucked the fabric out of the air. He waved it toward where she stood, paused to examine the pretty thing a bit more closely, and then spurred back toward the rest of his troop. After a brief consultation the whole band turned to hurry away.

"How marvelous!" said Floripas.

"How dreadful you mean," said Maragonde. "I think your husband to be may have words for you about that scarf."

Floripas seemed not to hear. "How splendid!" she said.

At the top of the great ramp a horn sounded. The city gate opened and her Uncle Corsuble led a charge of 50,000 men down the mighty road toward the plain. Floripas leaned her elbows on the wall to watch.

GUY DISPLAYED the scarf for Dukes Richard and Thierry. "Have you ever seen a fabric so fine? Or embroidery so fair?"

"Saracen silk," said Duke Thierry, "or I am a heathen myself. The needlework is Saracen too. I've never seen a more lovely form, but whoever that maiden was she is no Christian. This explains it all. The city has fallen, and we are in the jaws of a trap!"

A great brass horn sounded even as they turned their mounts toward the rest of their twelve thousand knights and squires. Fifty thousand Saracens came racing down the road from the open gates of Rome to intercept them.

"Now is the time for speed." said Duke Richard. "Someone must escape to warn King Charles!"

CORSUBLE, General and Uncle to the Lord High Admiral and Sultan of Spain, spared a brief curse for the ways of women before setting the incident aside from his mind. The trap had been well laid. The enemy might have escaped from the snapping jaws, but he still had to deal with the lion's pounce! All that remained was the contest of arms – and after a thousand victories in a hundred wars, Corsuble knew how to win. Speed and shock were his means and his tools. They had never failed him before, and they would not fail him now.

He stood in his stirrups, sounded his horn, and waved for his men to follow.

The battle that followed surpassed all this Roman field had seen in its months of recent war. The Saracens dashed forward with howls of challenge and cries of victory. Any other foe would have been swept from the field, but this was the guard of Charlemagne and the household troops of Normandy and Ardennes. No braver men could be found in all of France. Nor, as mattered more in this moment of peril, any knights with more discipline on the field.

By habit and training the French had waited in ranks while their lords rode off to explore. Now they lowered their lances as if bound by a single hand, and then spurred forward to challenge the foe. The ferocity and surprise of their counterattack broke the enemy lines just before the French commanders could be caught and surrounded.

Thereafter the field descended toward chaos, with bouts and small melees swirling in every direction. King Iblis fought always at the heart of the battle, crying insults and threats at all around.

Say what you will about his manner and pride, but Iblis in war was terrible to behold and doughty enough to battle the pride of France on even terms. But now, of course, he had to do that very thing. He was used to sweeping men from the saddle, and dominating as many as five or six foes at once. Not today. Every single soldier he faced seemed as tough to chew as a piece of old leather.

Corsuble was likewise astonished at the quality of the men he faced. He had hoped that the mere sight of so great a Saracen army would break the will of the French. They were but scouts, after all, and knew they had no support. Failing that, he had counted on fear and hesitation to bring him an easy victory.

That ten thousand men might charge as one into the teeth of five times their number had simply never occurred to him. *"This Charles may deserve his reputation after all,"* he said to himself. *"But no army survives without its leaders. Smite off the head and the body will fall to pieces."*

He paused to survey the field and then charged toward the brightest and highest of the noble French banners – the Golden Lions of Normandy on their field of crimson red. Duke Richard sallied forth to meet him.

The two champions met with a shock that amazed all who fought nearby, and shattered their lances into darts of shrapnel that buzzed through the air like bees. Both knights reeled in their saddles, but neither man fell.

Moving in eerie rhythm they each drew sword and charged at the foe again. Corsuble's curved blade met Richard's with a resounding *'clang!'* Then the Frenchman took control of the fight.

Subtle signs from knee and foot caused his charger to rear, brushing the enemy's sword aside and lashing out with steel-shod hooves stronger than any mace. Corsuble barely managed to intervene with his shield, which rang like a bell at Matins, and staggered back in fear for his life. Richard pursued, causing his mount to prance forward, still on two legs, striking again and again. Corsuble was forced to turn his back and flee, which opened his guard to a cut that sent the Saracen's visor spinning away through the sky.

"Hah!" said the Frenchman. "You were passing lucky to keep your head. Come try me again so I may finish the job!"

Corsuble instead backed away to a safe distance and then bowed in his saddle, his scimitar pressed to his chest in the Saracen gesture of respect.

"I can only agree, Sir Knight. That was the finest display of horsemanship it's ever been my pleasure to see. I salute you!

"I am Corsuble, general of armies and Uncle to Balan; he who is the Admiral of Spain and Sultan of High Baghdad. 'Twas I who taught the mighty Fierabras his craft, so I know of what I speak.

"Your name I can guess already. Who could you be but Duke Richard of Normandy? Your fame precedes you! Now I will bear witness to any and all that you earned it."

Now it was Richard's turn to bow in the saddle. Corsuble continued.

"It would break my heart to see you dead on this field Sir Richard. Look about you. The trap has shut. Surrender now and upon my honor you will be held in a captivity so rich that any king or prince would envy your life. I will also guarantee that your commonest soldier dines on meat from the bone. Their courage deserves no less. But none of this can come to pass unless you surrender. Why waste lives when you have no hope? It is folly."

"Do not count your ransom yet," said Richard. "You speak of Norman wolves, and rejoicing about the cage is folly until you stand outside the door! Raise your sword, heathen. I have other tasks to attend to this day."

"As you wish," said Corsuble. He urged his mount forward and set his sword to dance.

Now it was Richard's turn to stare in amazement. The curved Saracen blade twisted, twined, and hissed through the air so fast that even the eye of a paladin could see naught but silver arcs going by. Worse yet, that silver was Damascus steel and sharper than the edge of a minstrel's wit! The cuts fell like rain on Richard's defense, sending bits of his shield flying in all directions. Worse, he found it all but impossible to return the strokes. Whenever he raised his own sword, Corsuble's keen edge would pin it down, or his darting point would flash toward a gap the Frenchman had to protect.

Richard sought to renew his earlier success and signaled for his horse to rear. Before it could, however, the Saracen pushed in close and laid his edge on the charger's chin.

"No, no," he said. "We'll have no more of that! I have no wish to slay your steed. But I will if you force me."

Duke Richard could only stare with rounded eyes. Then, before he could voice a reply, the razor edge flicked away from the horse's neck and flashed once more toward the rider's face. Richard barely had time to duck his head to take the blow on his helm instead. That action saved his life, but it was a full heavy stroke that nevertheless caused blood to stream from the Frenchman's nose. A second cut followed, slicing clean through the aventail that hung from his helm and carving deep into the gorget that protected his throat. A gnat's hair deeper and the Duke of Normandy would have died on the spot.

Richard reeled away, only to be pursued by a third hard stroke, and then a fourth that caved in his visor above one eye. Desperate now, and all but blind, he thrust upward toward where he could only suppose his foe to be waiting. Corsuble was ready. The deadly curved blade circled around Richard's own, caught it in a lock, and then twisted the hilt from his grasp.

With nothing else to do, Richard leapt from his stirrups and threw his arms around the Saracen's neck like a lovelorn bride on her wedding night. Then he fell from the saddle, taking his opponent down with him.

Paladin though he was, Richard hit the ground like an awkward child. He lay for a moment half stunned. Even worse, when his eyes finally focused he still couldn't see because of the damage done to his visor. He rolled away in a full panic, tugging and pulling to get his helmet off while his breath bounced back from imprisoning steel, hot, wet and heavy. Finally – *finally* – the helm came away. Richard drew in a long breath of cool, fresh air and then looked up, fully expecting to discover a sword pressed to his neck. It wasn't there. Corsuble lay where he'd fallen. The general's neck had snapped when the pair of them struck the ground.

GUY OF BURGUNDY rode up and dismounted with a single, fluid motion to stand by Richard's side. He caught the older man by both shoulders and gave him a tight embrace.

"Your Grace, are you well? I saw your struggle but it took me some time to break free. I must admit – I thought the worst when I saw you fall."

He nudged at Corsuble's body with his toe and said, "It looks like this villain suffered the fate I feared for you. May God damn his heathen soul to hell!"

Duke Richard shoved Guy roughly away. "Villain? Say not so! That was the finest swordsman I've ever faced. He had me, Guy. As I am a man and a knight, this Saracen had me beat. Only blind, stupid luck was enough to save me."

"Luck? Say not so. Surely this was the hand of God."

"I am no priest who can tell the difference. All I'll say is this: if God has room in heaven for my sinner's soul, I hope he can make room for this man's too!"

Guy said nothing. He merely watched in silence as Richard cast about for an unbroken spear to plant by the dead man's head with Corsuble's banner tied to the top as a makeshift flag. The curved sword went on the Saracen's breast in the same gesture of respect that Corsuble had made but a bare few minutes before.

Then the Duke of Normandy took up his own blade from where it had fallen and climbed nimbly back to the saddle, bareheaded but ready for more.

"Come Guy. The enemy has withdrawn for the moment. Sound your horn and summon the men. We'd best retreat while we can."

SO ENDED the final battle of Rome for that ill fated year. The Saracens were full dismayed at the sight of their General's end, just enough for the French to fight their way free in the confusion that followed. Two thousand men lay dead on the field behind them.

Many a man wept through the night when the French finally set camp. No one felt sorrier than Guy himself. He said to the other Paladins, "This was my first command and it has led to nothing but death and defeat."

"Say not so," said William the Scot. "Roland himself could have done no more than you accomplished this day. We came too late. By some treason or guile they had mastered the city already. Their trap was well laid, but we managed to escape it. Wherein do you find any failure?"

Duke Thierry and Duke Richard agreed. "Above all we have performed our most important task. The report is sent, and the King will be forewarned. There is nothing left for us to do but abide until Charles arrives."

KING CHARLES had left nothing behind when he gathered his army for the rescue of Rome. All the Twelve Peers had come to his summons, with a hundred thousand soldiers at their side. Sir Roland led the vanguard, while brave Oliver patrolled behind to guard the rear. The King and his barons rode with the middle party under Charlemagne's famous banner, the Oriflamme of St. Denis and France.

Sir Guy and his force met them at the road leading down from the pass. After relating his own tale yet again, the young knight described how the Sultan had burnt, pillaged, stolen and enslaved all he could find of the Christian faith. Guy also spoke of the threats that Iblis had made in the heat of battle: vows that the Sultan would mount another invasion *'to seek out Charles in his rat-holes'* and do even worse to the people of France.

"God forbid he ever dare!" cursed Guy, his eyes filled with tears once again.

Charles laid a hand on the young man's shoulder. "His search will take but little time. He'll find Us soon enough, you may be sure! And then he and Balan alike will pay for all their evil work. I swear it by God and Saint Denis! I shall pursue them both forever, be they within walls or without. There will be no mercy; save only if they come to be baptized and abandon their heathen ways."

CHAPTER 5 – CHECKED BY THE GIANT MAMBRINO

The King barely had time to reestablish order in the city of Rome before word came of a new Moorish army that had crossed the Pyrenees to pillage in France itself. This time Charles was determined to catch the enemy before they could escape. He called Duke Basyn of Bordeaux into his court.

"These are your lands that have been invaded," said Charles. "Your men deserve to lead our response. Go forth, find them, and hold them until We arrive with the rest of the army. I can lend you 15,000 knights to help, but you will still be outnumbered. I therefore expressly require and command that you *only* hold them. Waste no lives in pursuit of vengeance! There shall be justice aplenty, I promise, when the rest of Our army arrives."

Thus the French set forth with the noble Duke racing ahead on swift horses and the royal army marching in his wake. The King made good time. Three weeks was enough to see them camped in hills that would rise the next day to become the Pyrenees. Riders found them that evening.

"Sire," they called. "Grief is upon us! A giant holds the bridge against us. He has felled Duke Basyn and many others beside. We cannot cross!"

Charlemagne and his Paladins hurried ahead through the night, leaving the army to follow. Clambering over trails that would have shamed a goat, they arrived on the scene just as the morning sun began to paint the peaks with a palette of pink and gold.

Before them lay a chasm so deep that wind moaned through its walls like an army of fallen souls, and the river at its bottom seemed like a thin, blue thread in the distance. A magnificent bridge spanned the way, two bowshots long and wide enough for ten men to march abreast. It too seemed slender to the eye compared to the vast space beneath.

The bridge ended at a clearing on the far side of the gorge. Across the clearing lay a road that descended in easy stages down to the fields of Spain. The clearing's center held a single, full-grown oak, and beside that a massive boulder.

Duke Basyn's men sat on the near side of the bridge. Their camp was neat, clean, and filled with men who seemed to be drowsing in peaceable comfort by their fires.

Charlemagne spurred down the hill in wrath. "Who commands here?" he cried.

The soldiers brought forth a litter that held a bachelor knight in the livery of Bordeaux. Both his legs were broken, his right arm lay in a sling, and a heavy pall of pain and defeat could be seen in his expression. His eyes filled with tears as he spoke.

"Sire, ours is a tale of woe. We arrived at this cursed bridge but a scant hour behind the Moorish host. We saw their banners descending yonder road, and my lord commanded us to sound our horns so the heathen might know the Arm of France had arrived to deal him justice! He led the way to this infamous bridge. But then... Look you there, beneath that tree."

The knight pointed across the chasm. The King followed with his eye, and then gasped.

"A giant!" For indeed it was, seated half out of sight with his back against the great stone.

"Aye," said the knight bitterly. "But say rather a monster. A monster that felled my lord in less time than it takes to speak of it and imprisoned him beneath that stone. When His Grace fell twelve of us took saddle and charged to his rescue. We were destroyed in half as many seconds. Four lie caged with my lord. The others are... below." He nodded to the chasm. "I was the last. He took me out of the saddle like a boy snatching a ball, and then cast me across the bridge. My fall unhorsed two more of our knights. He laughed at that. I shan't ever forget that sound."

"The next day, fifty followed to a similar fate. The day after that a hundred! But all to no avail. His skin is like stone and we could make no dint.

"Sire, the giant says his name is Mambrino. He boasts of fell deeds performed at Rome and claims to be invincible. I fear we shall never see my lord again."

"There you are wrong." This came from Ogier the Dane. "Fear not Your Majesty. Such beasts are not unknown in my far off land to the north. We have learned how to deal with them."

So saying he strode to his horse and retrieved his great Danish war axe. This was a hideous weapon, five feet long with a huge, steel head forged by Wieland himself, the Dwarvish smith of Saxony. In Ogier's hands it seemed almost a toy. No knight in Charlemagne's court even approached the Dane when it came to stature alone. Seven feet tall and 300 pounds, Ogier towered above them all. And it wasn't just size. Every inch and ounce of the man was agile, graceful and incredibly strong. Axe in hand, this marvel among knights strode out upon the bridge.

The giant stood to face him, and a moan of dismay passed over the army.

Men had sometimes called Ogier a giant. Now their folly could be seen for what it was. Next to Mambrino even Ogier was but a child; puny and insignificant. His legs were like trees and his arms as thick as barrels. Just as frightening in an eerie way, he wore no clothes save a pair of massive trews, and no armor save a shining, golden, featureless helm. Nor did he carry a weapon. Neither sword nor spear was there to be seen. But he came with a menace that nevertheless set the bravest of men atremble.

Ogier marched forward, undaunted. "Giant! You have imprisoned my friend and bar the path of my King. Release your captives and be off – or take up your arms and pay the price to Ogier the Dane!"

The giant laughed; a low, slow, deep sound that echoed through the chasm. "FOOOOOOL. MAMBRINO NEEDS NO WEAPON TO DEAL WITH THE LIKES OF YOU."

Ogier made no answer. Instead he stepped from the bridge and began to swing his great axe. First this way, then that; over and over, round and round, in a great figure-eight. The giant spread his arms and came closer but Ogier never moved except to push his axe faster and faster. Finally, just as the giant loomed above him and raised a hand, Ogier shifted his weight and drove the great blade forward, with all that pent up force, right into the monster's belly. Where it stopped – harmless.

Ogier's eyes widened with shock. The giant's mocking laugh boomed across the gorge. Then he lashed out, caught the knight up, and tucked him beneath one massive arm like a squirming child. Ogier struggled to no avail. Mambrino carried him to the boulder, rolled it aside with one hand, and then tossed the hero down with his other captives. The whole encounter hadn't lasted to a count of ten. And the only evidence that remained was the low, grinding sound of the moving stone as it shut off the paladin's protests mid-word.

"So it went with my lord," said the wounded knight. A new stream of tears poured down his cheeks.

IT WAS OLIVER who broke the silence. "Sire, I claim the right to rescue our fallen peers."

The King protested, but Oliver would not be gainsaid. He drew his sword and strode proudly across the bridge. The giant watched him coming and then spoke as the knight set foot onto land.

"MAMBRINO WEARIES OF THIS." He launched a blow that would surely have felled a tree, but there was no knight there to receive it. Oliver slipped to one side, striking three hard blows at knee, shin and ankle as the foe swept past. Loud *"thwacks!"* echoed like drumbeats in the canyon. Mambrino whirled and grabbed, but caught only air as Oliver tumbled out of reach, coming up low and ready.

Again and again the dance repeated. Mambrino stalked, or charged, or leapt at his smaller foe. Oliver dodged nimbly aside, slashing with cut after cut that went unnoticed. Time passed. The giant grew ever more angry. Finally he let out a roar of frustration and stood straight up, towering up to his fullest height.

Oliver darted in, striking at the open target. But this time Mambrino had a plan. He raised his foot and slammed it down so hard that the earth trembled and shook. Oliver, caught in mid-lunge, stumbled to the ground.

The giant pounced, his teeth bared and wolfish. He grabbed the knight with a single hand, raised him up, and then smashed him down to the earth.

Oliver moved no more. Mambrino stayed where he was for a long moment, chest heaving. Then, with great deliberation, he raised his foot and kicked the unconscious knight across the field, to slam against the boulder. Mambrino followed, rolled it aside, and then tipped Oliver into the pit to join his other victims. The stone made a thick, sickening sound as it ground back into place.

At this disgraceful act thirty thousand eyes turned away in sorrow and shame, but those of Roland narrowed and flamed. His great sword Durandal leapt into his hand, and then the greatest knight in all the world stepped out upon the bridge.

Roland was Charlemagne's favorite knight; his champion, and his nephew beside. But there is about a knight – certain knights, at certain times – a peculiar air of magnificence. And when that air came upon Roland, even Charlemagne stood aside. As he did now.

Mambrino charged with a snarl, hurling a fist the size of a normal man's chest. Again there was no knight there to receive it. But this time there was a sword. Durandal smacked the monstrous fist with a sharp crack that echoed between the canyon walls.

"AHHHH!" The giant staggered back, eyes wide with shock and out-rage. He put his hand to his mouth, sucked at the knuckles, and glared at his miniature foe. Then he began to advance once more.

Just as Oliver had done, Roland wove a pattern of confusion, strik-ing high and low so fast that his blade hummed and blurred in the sun. Before long, the giant was again gasping with fury and frustration. But this time there was a difference, for no matter how he stormed or stamped, growled or grappled, Roland was the wind. When the earth shook with Mambrino' rage, Roland glided above it; when the giant pawed with his huge hands, Roland slid beneath; when the giant struck, Roland stepped nimbly aside.

Time passed and Mambrino began to strain. Eventually his breath began to rasp like a bellows. A few minutes after that he staggered. Finally he stopped, and just stood there gasping.

"YOU FIGHT ... GOOD," he managed, "BUT MAMBRINO WILL REST NOW."

The words were out of Roland's mouth before the slightest thought; the only words he could ever have said.

"But of course. Take as long as you like."

The giant sat with a heavy crash, sucking in great gulps of air. "YOU FIGHT GOOD," he said again. "BUT YOU CANNOT BEAT MAMBRINO. NO ONE CAN BEAT MAMBRINO. GO BACK."

Roland said nothing.

"BUT ALL MEN LOSE TO MAMBRINO! LOOK." The giant held forth his hand so Roland could see a thin, red line where Durandal had struck the knuckles. "YOU CAN DO NO WORSE. GO BACK."

Roland again said nothing.

"THEN YOU WILL DIE!" The giant's snarl echoed through the chasm, loosing a rain of stones that rattled down the walls. "MAMBRINO WILL TEAR OFF YOUR ARMS LIKE WINGS FROM A CHICKEN!"

Roland merely sighed and looked away. His shoulders dipped with fatigue. Now that they'd paused, he felt the shock of every blow that had glanced from the rocklike hide. Worse, the long, sleepless night descended on him like a heavy blanket of sodden wool. A great weariness bowed his head. His stomach growled.

MAMBRINO drew in buckets of air with each breath. Roland, glancing up, could see the arrogance slowly return to the giant's eye. The huge muscles rippled subtly even in stillness, shifting beneath skin that was covered with a multitude of tiny scratches. For indeed the giant was not unmarked. Rather, he bore many signs of the day's adventure. They were all small, like the marks a man might receive from a bramble, but there nevertheless.

Perhaps ten minutes passed with the giant slowly catching his breath, and the Paladin lost in thought. Then Mambrino leapt to his feet with a sudden roar and charged at his tiny foe. Roland tumbled aside, drew Durandal, and the deadly dance began again.

But now things were different. Refreshed, the giant moved faster than before, while Roland's leaden weariness persisted. His limbs ached. What had been an arm's length of safety shrank to the space of a hand, and then to no more than a finger. Wind from the giant's fist shook Roland's mail like cloth in a breeze.

Then came the moment when the knight moved too slow. One of the giant's fingers brushed against Roland's shoulder and sent him tumbling off balance. He leaned on his sword to rise but Mambrino was there too fast. A backhanded slap threw him tumbling toward the edge of the cliff.

"MAMBRINO TOLD YOU: HE CANNOT BE DEFEATED! YOU WOULD NOT LISTEN. SO NOW YOU MUST DIE."

One knee down, and one up, struggling to stand, Roland shook his head in an effort to collect his scattered senses. He forced his eyes to focus – to probe his advancing foe – and that was when it happened. As sometimes occurs for the greatest of knights everything went... slow. The world took on an uncanny distinctness. As the giant laughed in triumph, Roland watched how every breath and sound sent a tiny quiver across the hard, gray skin.

He saw the sweat pooling on the muscled chest. He saw a bead of it break free to trickle down the massive front. And then he saw the bead stop, and turn sideways – caught in the scratch made by Ogier's axe. A scratch that was deeper than all the others. And that was all it took for Roland to see what had to be done.

Mambrino reached down but the knight tumbled aside as he'd done so many times before. Durandal soared, and dove, and then struck – scraping along Ogier's mark like a thread hurled through the eye of a needle. The giant snarled and snatched another time, and again Roland was a wisp while Durandal flew: in, across, and out, precise enough to cut that selfsame thread in half along its length.

Time passed, but time no longer had meaning. There was only the sun, the air, the steps, and the cut. In, across, and out.

How long did it take? No one can say for sure, but the sun was low when the giant suddenly winced in pain and fell still. A puzzled look appeared on his face and he reached to his side. The horny hand came back red with blood. He gazed at it in shock. "THIS CANNOT BE. I AM MAMBRINO!"

Roland said nothing.

With a cry that deafened the onlookers, the monster spun away toward the oak at the center of the clearing. He wrenched it from the ground with a mighty cry and then stripped it of branches like a man might strip a branch of twigs – running his hand down the trunk and snapping them off at the base. Then he broke the trunk over his knee, threw the unwanted piece at Roland and charged with a roar, swinging wildly.

Roland dove aside. Mambrino followed, sweeping fierce, tireless blows back and forth. Roland dodged again, first to the left, then to the right, and then forced to retreat. Finally he saw an opening and struck. Durandal snaked out and cracked on the giant's knuckles just where it had before. Mambrino dropped his club. And then Roland was on him.

Durandal soared and stooped like a silver hawk. In, across, and out.

Once, and the giant staggered. Again, and he fell to his knees. And then a final time: a mighty two-handed blow that drove Mambrino to measure his length in the dust.

The golden helmet popped free and slowly rolled away to tumble over the cliff. Blood poured steadily from the wound – still no wider than a hair, but deep enough at last.

UTTER SILENCE gripped the chasm for a long, still moment. Then a lone voice rose up with a jubilant cry. Others joined it until a great cheer echoed and danced between the walls. Men poured over the bridge like the tide in search of a shore. Twenty were needed to heave the boulder aside. Ladders were brought to help Ogier, Oliver and the other prisoners climb out into the failing light. All men were filled with joy and celebration. All save for the King.

Charlemagne strode to the edge of the clearing to gaze down the road toward the sunny fields of Spain. No army was there to be seen. Roland came up beside him.

"It is too late, your Majesty. Is it not." This was both observation and question.

"Aye Roland, I fear it is. By now they're hid behind wall and moat. Much work it will take to dig them out. More, I fear, than the weather will allow.

"But this much I swear," he said, turning to face his nephew. "This I swear on the honor you've won today. When the snows have faded and the green buds stir, you and I shall stand here again. We and all our friends. And on that day Admiral will pay sixfold and more for all the evil he has done. You have the word of Charles!"

CHAPTER 6 – ASSAULT INTO SPAIN

Winter did as winter will, hemming inside both the villain and the virtuous alike. The Saracens passed the time enjoying the fruits and memories of their triumphant year. The French spent it laying their plans for revenge.

Charlemagne heard his Easter mass at Aix and then set off for Spain even as the bees began their busy rounds. The army marched through the pass of Montalban, where ill-starred Renaud had built his famous keep, and thence down to the land of Spain.

They took the castle that guarded the Saracen side of the pass by a single great assault. Neither tower nor town survived the day. The vengeful French burnt and slew all that they found, leaving nothing higher than the knee of a half-grown boy. Man and woman, child and dog, crops and cattle alike. Everything they found, they slew.

Tidings went swiftly to Admiral Balan of the coming of Charles with all his Twelve Peers. The Admiral also heard in great detail of the hundred thousand bachelor knights, stout and gay, who rode at the side of the Christian King.

"This is a wonder!" Balan said. "How dare he be so bold? Has he no notion of the power he faces? This 'Emperor' of France may dread me little now, but he shall be taught a proper respect before he departs! I swear it by Mahon's eyes."

The Sultan sent ambassadors to provinces far and near; to towns, cities, castles and towers in all the lands of his realm and sway. "Come to me!" he called. "Come from India and Asia; Phrygia and Ethiopia; from Nubia, Turkey and Barbary; Macedonia and Bulgaria; and from every corner of Spain. Come to me at Aygremore, and come to me ready for war!"

They answered in numbers. Three hundred thousand and more. Some were blue, some yellow, and some black as a Moor. Some were handsome of face and form. Others were as horrible and strong as a devil from hell. But each and all were fell and fatal warriors, and they swelled the Admiral's army beyond all count. He walked among them spreading his word.

"You, dear friends, are the bearers of my trust. You must avenge me on these French dogs. They have done me many a villainy. Many of my people have they slain. And now they menace my very throne and drive toward my country again. Together we shall offer their blood to Mahon and all of our Gods."

He made the soldiers drink the blood of wild beasts; of tiger, antelope and of giraffe, as is the custom of Saracens to stir their courage in the days before battle. The men stomped and screamed. Many foamed at the mouth and tore at their skin with their nails, leaving long red lines of blood that they licked from their fingers like beasts. But still the Sultan was not yet done.

An army of horns was blown and priests went down among the troops. They showered the men with silver and gold, and led them in song and chant. The idols they carried vanished and reappeared in the thick clouds of scented smoke. When the idols had passed each man went forward until he came to the foot of Balan's high throne, where every one made a solemn vow to avenge the Admiral's injury.

When all was done, Admiral Balan called in all his chiefs to council: King Iblis, King Sortibrant, and Fierabras the Strong; Mavone the Engineer, the Moorish King Brullant, and a score of lesser barons besides. "I charge you upon your allegiance. Bring me that wretch who calls himself the King of France. Bring him here to my pavilion. I want him alive. The rest of the French you may slay.

He motioned to Fierabras to join him by the throne. "My son shall lead the attack. Tomorrow, ere daybreak, he shall ride from the city with a hundred thousand of those who've lately come; Asians, Phrygians, Pagans, Turks, Indians and Venetians, Barbarians, Ethiopians and Macedonians."

He turned then, and spoke to his son directly. "Charles I want alive. Him I shall keep to teach a bit of courtesy. Of the others leave nothing. All are to be slain, especially the Twelve Peers – saving only Roland and Oliver who bear such great renown. Them you may spare, but only if they will deny their Gods and agree to worship Mahon and Termagant."

Fierabras immediately arrayed himself for battle and rode forth with a strong army to give the first battle. They made their camp at the fortress of Mantryble, the only means by which the great River Flagot could be crossed for a hundred miles in either direction. When word arrived that the French approached, the Saracens rode out to meet them.

THE ENCOUNTER began when Fierabras, with the 100,000 men of his advance guard, came upon a troop one-fifth that size under the command of Roland, Oliver, and young Guy of Burgundy. The land was such a maze of twisting creeks, sharp hills, and dense copses that neither side could truly guess at the other's true size. That caused no delay in the onset of battle.

The two chieftains met at the head of their charging forces. Roland struck first, laying a spear thrust on Fierabras' shield that left him gaping like a man astounded, and struggling to cling to his saddle. Fierabras sought to fight back but received a second blow, this time on his helm, which left him stunned and aimless. It felt like his eyes were on fire. He might have died then and there had the press not swept them apart.

Sir Iblis met with Oliver and hit him on the shield with a stroke that was right well set. A quarter of the Paladin's shield spun off and flew over the field. The press drove them apart before Oliver could reply.

Thus they hurtled together all the day, now hither and now thither. Many a horse went astray. Many a good knight fell. But the valor of the French and the numbers of the heathen opposed each other in such perfect balance that neither could gain an advantage.

This changed at the moment when Charlemagne arrived with the rest of his army. It should have been a moment of triumph, and it did win the field at the end, but only at a terrible price.

The flow of battle had contrived to place Roland at the top of a hill with Oliver in a dell some distance away. The combat had been fierce and hot at both these spots throughout the day. Oliver's horse had been slain beneath him, and he'd yet to find a remount when the sight of Charlemagne and the Oriflamme sent a mass of the enemy into terrified flight. The King was right happy to see their backs, but might have felt differently if he'd known their path led right over the top of His most chivalrous knight.

Resisting such a tide of men and mounts was like standing in the path of an avalanche. Oliver could do nothing but curl in a ball and pray that the strength of his armor and the grace of the Lord would be enough to see him through. Sharp edged hooves battered him from all directions. Arrows from the attacking French rained down as well, and one ill-fated bolt pierced through his thigh just below the hip. Another stuck in his visor like a quill standing in a pot of ink. The razor-edged point quivered less than an inch away from his eye. He sat and yanked the thing free only to be struck squarely in the back of his helm by a Saracen mace, and then by a score of Saracen hoofs. Their panicked flight sounded like thunder in Oliver's ears. He was long beyond hearing before even their vanguard had passed.

From his height on the hill Roland saw the danger and charged down to help. Durandal in hand, he forced his way through the retreating enemy, fierce as a lion and smiting with all his power at any who came within reach. Forty of the heathens died so swiftly that their fall seemed like the opening petals of a gigantic flower. The sight put such great doubt in the Saracen hearts that the mass diverted their flight toward different paths.

Roland stood like a rock in the midst of the river, slaying all who ventured too close. His stance never changed for a moment until the knights of Atri arrived to help both Oliver and his guardian back to safety and aid.

IT WAS CLEAR that the French would hold this field at the end of the day from the moment Charlemagne arrived, but such were the Saracen numbers and the skill of their leaders that it was still no easy contest.

The Twelve Peers fought with their accustomed skill. The swords of Duke Naymon and Ogier accounted for dozens at least, as did those of Guy and Duke Basyn. But Fierabras was ever about to prevent the retreat from becoming a rout.

At length King Charles saw Fierabras rallying the Saracen troops and set his spurs to charge. He drew Joyeuse and with his own hand threw thirty Saracens dead upon the well churned field of stone and mud. Then he descended on the giant with a mace and struck his helm so hard that Fierabras was wild for rage and woe. The press made it impossible for him to return the blow, however, and he was forced to retreat with his men.

Sir Iblis of Samarkand then pressed to Charlemagne's side. "Sir, with hard luck have you been graced today. I have promised the Sultan to bring you to him and the Twelve Peers all. Now shall we depart from thy kin and in to the Admiral's hall. Yield to me if your life you would save!"

Charles replied with his sword. He laid a stroke on the pagan's helm that sent the man to raving words that made even less sense than the ones he'd just spoken. Had he been alone, Iblis would have been another life laid to the Emperor's tally. But he was not. The men of Samarkand rushed in a throng to rescue their lord with a host of Nubians and Turks at their side.

Now it was Charlemagne who found himself imperiled. Duke Naymon, Duke Ganelon, and Oliver's father Duke Reyner fought to his side, which afforded a space of safety until some of the other paladins could arrive. First came Richard of Normandy, roaring through the press and striking down foes to both left and right. Then Sir Aimery of Rome with William the Scot. Together, the little band pressed forth toward freedom. The Saracens resisted, knowing their only hope lay in capturing or slaying the King and his barons. A brief but titanic struggle engulfed the hilltop until Ogier and Duke Thierry entered the fray as well. The enemy broke for a final time.

The French had fought with such faith and force that the field was packed beyond measure with corpses by the time it grew dark. Thirty thousand Saracens had lost their need for a nightly bed.

ALL THINGS must have an end. Night came on and the parties drew apart.

Fierabras spoke to his army as it gathered back together by the Bridge of Aygremore. "Let our horns be blown to end this dreadful day. This battle was so sharp that many a man and wife have cause to pale at its name. And in truth our gods have been no help. What devil could it be that ails them?

"I shall never know peace in my heart until I have redress for the shame I now feel! I must prove my might on Roland, or on Oliver that was so quick and nimble. The evil of this day came by their hand; I shall not rest until I've been crowned as King in Paris despite them all!

"Oh red Mars omnipotent, hear my plea on your throne in the vaulted sky! You are the god of battle and granter of victory in arms. Grant me a noble combat against these men. To secure it I will offer up a crown of precious stones each year on your holy day, and see your temples dressed with myrrh and frankincense each week on the Tuesday that bears your name.

"Only give to me victory over these Christian dogs! Allow me to slay them like the pigs they are, to repay tenfold the destruction and wrongs they have done to my men. Great Mahon, give them mischance and give me a chance for glory!"

ROLAND Felt no more joy than Fierabras that evening. His thoughts had grown ever darker as he followed the litter with Oliver's limp form back toward the camp. His friend's armor was so battered and dented that it had to be cut off piece by piece. A blacksmith had to be summoned to deal with the helm, greaves and vambraces, all of which were crushed so tight to the paladin's form that only shears could remove them. If the truth be told, Roland fretted worse than Duke Reyner, for all the gray-haired man was Oliver's own father.

Neither one left Oliver's side until Bishop Turpin himself came to reassure them. "Fear not. He is battered and beaten, and I wouldn't want to be feeling his aches on the morrow, but there is nothing that time will not heal. Give him a week or two and he will be back in the fray and no worse for the wear."

WHILE FIERABRAS was bemoaning his losses and Roland was fearing the worst, King Charles was in his pavilion celebrating the day with honor and joy. The taste of triumph lay as sweet on his tongue as the cups of wine that graced his high table. Many were the words of praise he spoke.

First he gave thanks to almighty God and Saint Denis for their aid, and then to the Virgin for the comfort and courage with which She filled his soldiers' hearts. Of his men he gave particular praise to his older knights and commended the younger men to contemplate on their glory.

"Our young Peers fought with great courage today. But who was it that rode to their rescue in the end? None but those whom foolish souls have sometimes called too old! Was it my beloved nephew who won this day? Nay, it was not. Today the glory goes to we who have earned some gray in our beards. Look upon Our good Duke Basyn who rescued his son Sir Aubrey, and Duke Reyner who helped to save his Oliver. I saw Duke Thierry as well, leading a charge with his boy Gerard of Montdidier but a hand behind. Raise your cups and drink to the lessons that our elder knights still know how to teach!"

Roland entered the tent at the end of this with Bishop Turpin at his side. "How do you dare?" he demanded. "My dear friend Oliver lies wounded and insensible even now, and you sit here to your meal and make jokes while our backs are turned? Did we not do our duty today even as Your Majesty would have hoped?"

The King raised his cup again, this time toward the door.

"We saw you, good nephew. And we salute you too. You were as loyal and as fierce as any hen upon her roost, standing there to protect your friend! Nay, more than that - as any wolf upon her litter! And right glad We are that you did, for We are as fond of young Oliver as you. But would you deny the deeds of your elders, who won the day while you were so detained? Say not so, nephew. Come and join me in a cup of celebration!"

Roland was about to respond, and not with the kindest of words, but Bishop Turpin caught him by the arm and drew him outside instead.

"Peace, my son. Say no words now that you may regret in the morning."

"Me? How am I the one who should be regretting his words?" demanded Roland. "What have I said to make anyone complain?"

"Nothing. But I have little doubt that things might be different if I'd left you alone to say the words that were there on your face."

"Oliver nearly died!" said Roland. "To make shallow jokes on such a night is, is..." Words failed him.

Bishop Turpin raised a hand. "Being around your Uncle has made me a connoisseur of words that require some thought. This particular batch had a piquant tone, I thought: a bit harsh on the tongue, and red to the untutored eye. Aye, and lacking in their usual depth. Indeed, I'd say the words of this evening were no more deep than the grapes from which they arose."

Angry as he was, Roland had to smile at both the message itself and the way in which it was given. Turpin took the opportunity to guide the young man toward his bed.

CHAPTER 7 – OLIVER AND FIERABRAS

In the Saracen camp Fierabras made ready to uphold his oath. First his massive shield was repainted to hold a painting of Mars instead of Apollo. Then seven grooms were summoned to attend to his great black charger, and seven smiths to polish each and every one of the midnight scales that made up his magnificent armor. Fresh rubies were embedded in his adamantine helm, and Fierabras himself polished each of his three swords until they shone like miniature suns. Plourance he buckled to his belt. The other two hung from his saddle.

The Saracen prince secreted his men in a nearby wood and then continued forth alone. It wasn't long before he came upon the French lying in camp near a meadow.

"Where is the 'Emperor of Rome?'" he cried. "Where is this 'Charles'? Let him come forth and face me, or return to Paris to crawl on the floor with the beasts and brats of his Court! Or let him send a champion: Roland, Oliver, or Ogier the Dane. Or six champions! I will slay them all, or take them back to my father as captives. Tell the so-called King that the Admiral of Spain greets him with defiance."

He glared at the assembled French a moment longer, then turned his back and rode off to one of the solitary trees that dotted the plain. Once in the shade, he stripped off his armor and to all appearances relaxed to a casual nap.

King Charles motioned to a herald. "Who is this knight that makes so bold a challenge?"

"Sire, that is Fierabras, the prince who defeated young Sir Aimery in honorable combat before the siege of Rome. He is the son of the Admiral of Spain, but also a mighty ruler in his own right. He has slain at least ten different kings with his own hand, and taken from each his lands and possessions. By this means he now rules Russia, Alexandria, Arabia and all the lands to the East. He is also the lord of Jerusalem, the land of the Holy Sepulcher, and it was he who led the sack of Rome, slew the Pope, and spat down his headless neck. Truly, he is one of the mightiest and most admirable knights alive."

The King nodded slowly and then turned to the man at his right. "Dear nephew, prithee go slay me this heathen."

Roland struck a theatrical pose with his hand to his chest. "Sire! Surely you can't mean me. Don't you recall what you said last night?

"The heathen had ambushed us with 100,000 men in the afternoon, and we younger knights bore the brunt until you could arrive with the rest of the army. They wounded Oliver nigh unto death. Even now he lies sick abed. But last night you insisted on celebrating nevertheless – with a bit of food, a lot of wine, and a great many words.

"Everyone heard you. It went something like this: '*We old gray-beards had to rescue the youngsters because Roland was brooding over his broken egg like a hen on top of her nest.*' Very well! This seems the perfect chance to prove your point. Let one of your older knights go to face this pagan – for here is one youngster who won't."

Charles waxed mightily wroth at this defiance and slapped the younger man so hard that blood flew from Roland's nose. Durandal appeared in Roland's hand as if by magic, with the point held steady between him and the King. Men rushed to keep them apart.

"Sire!" said Ganelon. "Drawing steel on the King merits death."

"Death indeed." said Charles, "to draw on not only King, but Uncle as well. Seize him!"

"Nay, touch me not!" cried Roland. "He that tries I will cleave in twain."

Everyone froze in place. The moment stretched out until Ogier the Dane finally stepped slowly forth, his hands empty and open. "Roland. This is ill done. To bare steel against your lord and uncle?"

After a pause Roland answered, "Aye. You are right. I was sore provoked, but I repent me of the deed."

He sheathed his sword and marched to his tent. No one spoke until the flap had shut.

"This is an evil day," said the King. "First my champion threatens me, and still no one can be found to face this Saracen."

"Rest easy, Sire," said the wise Duke Naymon. "Another will surely appear."

But the King would not be comforted, and no one else stepped forth.

OLIVER STIRRED in his sickbed at the various cries outside. "What causes so great a commotion?" The answer left him horrified. "And no one has taken up the gauntlet? That will be fixed soon enough. Fetch my armor and sword." He rose from the bed and began to stretch.

"But you mustn't," said his oldest squire, a lad who had been knighted just months before. "Look! Your wounds have opened even from this."

"So? Bind them up and *then* get my armor."

"You have no armor, my lord. It had to be cut from your body. You cannot fight without armor!"

Oliver answered masterfully, speaking slowly and with an excruciating clarity. "Then fetch me your armor, bind these cuts, and dress me in that."

The boys could not resist. One squire brought lengths of clean linen while the others scurried off for arms and horse. The oozing stopped just as the armor arrived.

The boys protested again when the weight of the heavy mail sent a wave of tremors over the knight. "My lord, you must not do this!"

Oliver glared about impartially and turned to mount his horse alone. The effort surpassed his strength. "Help me here," he said.

Once more they had no choice. After a few sharp winces and a quickly stifled groan, they managed to raise him up to the saddle. He settled in with a satisfied sigh like a man coming home, and prodded his mount toward the still-raging King.

"Sire," he interrupted, "I beg a boon."

Charles spun about with wonder and joy. "Oliver! Most beloved of Earls, they said you'd be sick abed for at least a week. Name the boon and it's yours. There's not a castle or county in all my realm I wouldn't give you freely."

"That's not the sort of boon I meant. I wish to face this Saracen."

"Oliver, no! You are too ill. We all know how close you came to dying yesterday. How many savage wounds you received. And now you'd ride to an even greater danger? If you love me you will not ask this."

Oliver merely sat: poised, waiting and quietly insistent. Ganelon stepped forward.

"Sire," he said, "it is not the custom of France to deny a boon once promised. If this is what Count Oliver wants, it must be allowed. All we can do is pray for his triumph."

"This is evil counsel!" said the King. "What has the world come to when the law ordains that which lacks of honor? I swear by my troth that if this good knight should die or be taken, you and your line shall bear the sin!"

"I will trust in God to keep me," said Ganelon. *'And pray that Oliver never returns,'* he added to himself.

Fuming and full of regret, the King finally bowed his head. He hesitated a moment longer, then tossed his glove to Oliver. "May God and his angels keep you safe."

No sooner had the words been said than Duke Reyner, Oliver's father, arrived. "Sir King, have mercy. Take pity on my son and forbid this adventure!"

"I have tried Reyner, but it isn't mine to forbid. The boon was asked and granted. There's nothing else to be said."

"Please, Sire," said the Duke. He dropped to his knees and clutched the King's hand. "His are the words of presumptuous youth, driven by a desire to ever be over-courteous. Youth gives slight regard to perils and pains. It rests on we who are older and wiser to restrain it from hazarding its own destruction. Oliver took sore wounds but yesterday. Just look at him! Even now he pales from the loss of blood. You know how such a thing saps the stamina. You can't let him go. Not in this condition."

"Reyner, I may not gainsay that which I've granted. Oliver bears my glove, and seems well content with it. Direct your pleas to his ears, not mine."

The Duke covered his face and wept.

"Sir King," said Oliver from the saddle, "and all you barons. I beseech of you a gift. If I have in word or deed committed any sin against you, forgive me now and let me go with your pardon."

He turned his horse in the echoing silence and trotted off to the west. Many were the tears that followed.

The King called for Bishop Turpin and knelt to pray. His hands pressed together so hard that the knuckles showed white, and his eyes never left the paladin's dwindling form.

OLIVER FOUND the giant Fierabras a long mile from the assembled French, lying on his back beneath a tree. His hands were laced behind his head and he wore no armor, just a loose shirt that lay flat in the windless day. He smiled at the sight of an opponent and boomed out in a low, rumbling voice, "I wanted to fight a man, not some breast-high boy. Go back and send a real knight."

This he could say without jest, for Oliver would have barely reached that high had the giant been standing.

"You asked for a combat. I have come to provide one. If you find it too large to handle, I suppose I could find you a child with a wooden horse and a stick. Would that be more to your liking? Perhaps I should ask instead who it is that comes to my king with such arrogance?"

The giant chuckled. "You answer well! I am Fierabras of Alexandria, richest man in all the world and son of the Admiral of Spain. 'Twas I who sacked the city of Rome, slew your Pope, and bore away the treasures for which you take such pains. Jerusalem is also mine, and all the lands where your God was slain and buried long ago.

"Who are you that speaks so proudly?" he asked in turn.

"If but half of what you say is true, Pagan, you are an unhappy soul indeed. Take up your arms and defend yourself."

"First I would have your name and lineage; only then will you see me armed."

"You will have my name before the sun is set, that is sure. For now, be content to know that Charles, my King, has sent me to bear you these words: Give up Mahon and your other heathen idols, bow to the One True God, and be baptized. If you do, He will welcome you as a friend with open arms. If you fail, you must do battle with me. One or the other, the choice is yours, but you must give your answer now."

Fierabras gazed up at his foe with wonder. "Whoever you are, I marvel at your presumption – you may pay a dear price for it, by and by. Mighty kings have trembled to see me armed, and here you invite it! But first I would know more. This Charlemagne of yours, so renowned in many countries – what manner of man is he? Tell me too of Roland, Oliver, Ogier the Dane and all those other famous knights."

"You prattle on for no reason! But since you demand it, I will tell you that the Emperor Charles is of such great majesty that no man in all the world may compare to him in wealth, wisdom, or might. His nephew Roland is without peer; Oliver a little less than he; and as for the other Frenchmen, they are without doubt the most valiant people that ever was. But these words have no place here! Get up and arm yourself, or by God I will kill you where you lie."

A shadow crossed Fierabras' face. "I would strike you for such words but for the dishonor it would bring me."

"Strike ahead; I ask no more. Just get thee up and armed!"

"Do not worry," the giant said, "I can tell you're out of sorts and will not hold such words against you. Prithee, tell me now your name and line."

Oliver grit his jaw and answered tightly, "Very well. You may call me Garin. I was born to a humble man of Atri and have only that rank granted by the King, whom I serve for glory, love and hope of advancement. For which reason I insist that you take up your weapons, and rise to give me battle!"

Fierabras was outraged. "Where are Roland and Oliver? Where are Ogier, Thierry and all the other famous knights of the King? Why haven't they come to face me?"

"They did not deem you worthy. I am here instead and it is I you must fight – If you are hardy enough to meet me. But I swear by Saint Peter," Oliver finished, breathing heavily, "that if you do not arm yourself soon, I will run you through where you sit!"

Fierabras shook his head with regret. "Garin, I cannot. Since being dubbed a knight I have never jousted with any man less than a King, an

Earl, or a Baron of great valor. You come from a house too low for me to meet you in arms. It would be no honor to slay you. Besides, you seem a nice enough fellow.

"Let us do this instead. I shall let you strike me and will fall to the earth. When that happens, you can take my shield to King Charles and tell him that you vanquished me. You will thus gain your fame and riches, and I will be spared the need to kill you."

Oliver was furious. "I have another idea. Why don't I sever your head where you sit and *then* take your shield to the King?"

"I want nothing of you, Garin, but to return and send me Roland, Thierry, or one of the other knights of the King's high table. If none of them be hardy enough to come alone, send two or three at once; I care not and shall not refuse them." So saying, Fierabras lay back against the tree and closed his eyes.

Oliver bit back a scream of frustration. Instead, he twisted in the saddle and struck his fist against the bole of the tree. Green leaves fell like rain from the shock. "Do you *want* to be slain thus?"

The exertion opened some of the knight's wounds. Fierabras pointed to the blood dripping down Oliver's knee. "What's this? Your leg is hurt!"

"No it isn't," Oliver answered, kneeing his horse to move backward. "That's just chicken blood from my lunch."

"This is absurd! You're no match for me hale and sound – to slay you when you're wounded would only double the disgrace. Look you: hanging on the saddle of my horse are two flasks of potion from the Holy Land, the same with which your God was embalmed when he was taken down from the cross and laid in his grave. Go and drink one of the flasks. A single swallow will heal your wounds, both seen and hidden. Then you may defend yourself without danger."

"I'll do no such thing! I came here as foe, not guest."

"You are a fool without reason!" said Fierabras. "One day you'll come to regret it." Then he lay down and closed his eyes again. The sound of Oliver's grinding teeth filled the air.

SOME MINUTES passed before the giant spoke once more. "Tell me the truth, Garin. What manner of men are Roland, Oliver and the rest who have earned such fame and fear among the pagan folk?"

Oliver, having collected himself, answered in an even voice. "Roland, he is a little smaller than I, but only in stature. His courage is so great, his hand so heavy, and his heart so strong that he has no equal. No man alive can he face and fail to vanquish. As for Oliver, I judge that he is much like me in form and no better in greatness. The others vary as men will do, but all are valiant in their turn."

Fierabras' eyes gleamed eagerly. "By the faith I owe to Apollo and Termagant, I would not fear to face four such as you describe, nor would I leave the field until I'd slain them with my own sword."

At these words Oliver's patience finally snapped. He pointed his spear and made ready to strike the giant where he lay.

"Will you have no pity on yourself?" asked Fierabras. "If I rise as you ask and take my horse, not Charles and all your gods would save you from instant death. Were you but to see me standing, you'd be a brave man indeed not to tremble with fear."

"You have boasted too long of that which you never saw," Oliver said tightly. "It would suit you better to measure your speech. Too many lies may bring a man to mischief."

The giant's dark face twisted with anger and he rose to his feet in a single bound. He could look down at Oliver even though the knight was still mounted.

"In truth, I pity you Garin, for the noblesse of courage I see you bear. I give you this final chance to leave: go and send me Roland, or Oliver, or Ogier, or Gerard of Montdidier. I charge you expressly to say that I will abide here until they are ready to face me, and will not leave until I have conquered them one and all."

Oliver's face whitened, then flushed, and then whitened again. His fingers gripped the haft of his weapon so tightly that the wood seemed to groan beneath them. Had he not been the most honorable of knights, the giant would have perished there and then with a dozen wounds. But honorable he was, so he made no move to strike.

When Fierabras saw that he could not avoid the fight, he sighed. "Very well, be it on your own head. At least be so courteous as to come down and help me arm."

"Can I trust you?" Oliver asked.

"You may. I swear and assure you that I have never been traitor to any man, nor ever will."

Upon that promise Oliver stepped lightly down to the ground. First he held up the Saracen's heavy coat of Cappadocian leather. After that came the coat of black steel plates and finally the giant helm, which was richly ornamented with precious stones that flickered in the sunlight like stars.

Fierabras thanked him, and the two knights moved to their horses. In an eerie echo of the other's movements, each man took up a heavy lance of ash and steel, tossed it briefly for balance, then settled into the saddle. They seemed like two dancers hearing the same melody, or birds of the same flock that share an invisible tie. Fierabras hung the two vessels of holy balm on a rope about his neck.

"Garin, you are a right courteous knight, and gracious too. For the sake of the gentleness you have shown me I offer one more chance to return without fighting. I am not without pity for such valiant courage."

"Always you speak the greatest of follies," Oliver answered. "I shall never depart a field merely for fear of death or dismemberment. Nor is it I that should be afraid, for by the help of God it will be you that yields or dies ere the day is done."

Fierabras marveled again at the smaller man's mettle. "Then one final thing, good sir."

Oliver bit back a curse. "Speak it."

"By the cross on which your God was slain, the font where you were baptized, and your loyalty to Charles, Roland and the other Peers of France – I require that you give me your *true* name."

"You could adjure by no stronger things," Oliver admitted. "Very well. Know that I am Oliver, son of Duke Reyner, knight of the King, and close comrade of Roland the Strong."

"I knew that you could be no knight of little fame! Sir Oliver, it does me no honor to joust with a man half-dead already. Even now, I can see the blood dripping down your knee. Drink of this holy balm, or else retire to fight me when you are whole and sound. I will gladly wait on your convenience."

Oliver answered with a lowered lance. With a sigh, Fierabras did likewise. They charged as one while the King hid his face in fear.

THE KNIGHTS struck each other on the shield with such great force that both of the steel spearheads bent and bowed, the wooden shafts shattered, and fire sprang out on all sides. Sundered bits flew in all directions.

Oliver's horse dropped dead from the shock, while Fierabras' giant stallion staggered sideways and spilled his rider in a boneless heap. Both men wandered on foot, stunned and barely aware, until they chanced to come face to face. At the sight of a foe, they reached for their swords as one. Fierabras drew Plourance, Oliver the shining Hautclere, and they attacked.

The fight that followed was so fierce that the watching French cringed from the thunderous shocks even though they came from more than a mile away. Oliver landed the first telling blow, a stroke that sent jewels flying from Fierabras' helm like water shaken from a dog and then, still unspent, drove through the giant's shoulder plates and into the thick band of leather beneath. Fierabras' knees buckled and he staggered back, balancing with one hand on the ground. The French sighed to each other, "What a marvelous blow!"

Roland swore. "Would that it were me out there beneath Oliver's shield! I'd end this fight soon enough."

"Hah!" scoffed the King, "there speaks a felon coward. You make the offer now, but wasn't it you who refused this bout just a short time past? You won't forget that disgrace any time soon; not if I have anything to say about it."

"His Majesty shall do as He pleases," Roland answered coldly.

"Peace, both of you!" said Duke Naymon. "Let our prayers go forth in aid of Oliver, not against each other. The battle hasn't ended yet."

Naymon's words were prophetic. A second later Fierabras sidestepped a thrust and brought his sword down with a blow that split the corner from Oliver's iron shield, creased his helmet and still had enough force to spray links of mail in all directions.

The shock sent blood streaming from Oliver's many wounds, quickly soaking through the bandages. His leg, in particular, sagged beneath him so badly that he fell to the ground, shaking his head to clear his vision.

"God preserve me," he whispered, "what an evil stroke!"

Fierabras paused. "Now, at last, you know enough to fear. You are as brave a knight as I've ever met, Sir Oliver, but no one could fight with wounds like that. Go back; I would yet be content if you restored yourself before facing my full strength. You haven't felt it yet, I warn you. When my blood leaves my body it doubles my powers beyond all you have seen. But why continue at all? Charles cannot love you very much if he sends you forth in this condition. Why should you die in such a cause?"

Oliver's breath rasped as he answered. "All this time, Pagan, you have boasted how you would bring on the end of my days. I defy you now as I've done before. Slay me first, then vaunt of it."

He leaned on his sword and rose.

The knights rushed together again, smiting so furiously that buckles, rivets, plates, favors and precious stones were all hewn, broken and hurled to the ground. The two men disappeared in a fountain of metal bits, with sparks and fires that filled the air. The clamor made a deafening sound like a thousand smiths at the forge.

Across the field, King Charles looked away with tears in his eyes. "Oh Lord for whom we take such pains, preserve this good knight of mine and save him from death at the hand of this Pagan. If not, I swear by the soul of my father to leave not a church or altar or priest standing in all of France."

Naymon reproved him again, but the King made no reply.

THE TWO CHAMPIONS continued their battle with unequaled fierceness. Oliver pressed forward, raining down a flurry of blows that boomed on Fierabras' shield like a giant drum. Fierabras reeled back for a moment, then straightened and began to match the knight stroke for stroke. A sigh went through the assembled French as wonder stole even their fear away.

The fight balanced on a thread until Fierabras finally took the upper hand with one huge stroke that sheared the visor from Oliver's helmet, and then another that drove him face down to the earth. Oliver stood quickly, blood streaming down his ashen face, then dropped again as his injured leg gave way beneath him.

Fierabras stepped back from his fallen foe. "Sir Oliver, understand me. I have no wish to face you thus, when I have so great an advantage. Drink this flask of holy balm. It will make you whole and able to defend yourself properly."

"I'd rather die," Oliver gasped back. "I'll have nothing from you save that which I take in true combat."

He staggered to his feet and shakily raised his guard.

"You are obstinate beyond all reason!" Fierabras cried.

The giant reached back and threw an angry blow that would have hurled his opponent twenty feet if some miracle had prevented it from cutting through shield and body alike. Oliver saw it coming, however, and ducked beneath the deadly arc.

The force of the missed stroke pulled Fierabras off balance, creating the briefest of gaps in his guard. It was just enough. Hautclere thrust deep into the Saracen's thigh, then sharply drew back. Blood burst forth and stained the grass red for five feet in every direction.

Fierabras' eyes widened with shock and pain. He stumbled back against the tree, sagged a moment, then sat. He tugged urgently at the rope about his neck and raised a vessel to his lips.

Before the Frenchman's startled eyes, the wound closed and was instantly healed. Oliver staggered at the sight, reeling as if from some mighty blow. His face, pale and wan already, turned even grayer. But then he stubbornly gritted his teeth and moved in once again.

FIERABRAS met him stroke for stroke but Oliver's will had set. From some hidden source he seemed to recover a bit of his normal strength, and suddenly became a difficult target to hit. Whenever Fierabras set himself, Oliver shifted forward or back, striking and leaving from angles where Fierabras couldn't respond. When the giant spun to meet him, he darted across to another spot where he could strike but not be struck.

After a few minutes, though, his exhaustion showed in the sort of foolish mistake one might expect from a squire. His shoulder rolled forward with a thrust, overextending so that Hautclere snagged and caught on a bit of Fierabras' torn armor.

The Saracen reacted automatically. As every knight was taught, he clamped his shield arm close to pin the sword to his armored chest, and prepared a blow to finish the affair.

Oliver, who had planned the entire exchange, then committed an even more grievous martial sin. He dropped to his knees, yanked straight down to free the blade, and then leapt up with a hopeless thrust that that skidded across the giant's mail and stabbed the air by his shoulder. All Fierabras had to do was turn his head aside, and now Oliver was not only pinned but helplessly off balance as well.

Again the giant did exactly as they'd all been trained. He threw his opponent sprawling to the ground. The next step in the dance was for Fierabras to move in and either stake the knight to the earth or call for his surrender at sword point. Neither result occurred.

That foolish, hopeless thrust at the sky had not been meant as a blow. Instead, Oliver had used it to position Hautclere inside the rope around Fierabras' neck. When the giant hurled him down, the blade's keen edge severed the cord as cleanly as normal steel might cut through a piece of string. The last vessel of balm dropped and shattered at Fierabras' feet.

The giant gaped, stricken, at the broken flask. "You evil man! That potion was worth more than your weight in gold, and I'd have shared it with you gladly. Now you'll pay for it with your head!"

He hurtled forward but Oliver, once again on his feet, met the charge squarely and launched a flurry of cuts so fast that Hautclere vanished into a shining, silver blur. The stunned Saracen champion gave ground, first one step, then another, desperately trying to parry the attack.

It was Oliver's wounds that finally had the triumph. By now his blood was flowing so freely that little drops sprayed off with every blow he threw. His hand grew slick with it, and then numb from the constant impact. When his sword finally caught on the edge of Fierabras' iron shield, Oliver lacked the strength to hold on. Hautclere spun off across the field, leaving him empty handed.

More than ten thousand of the assembled French leapt for their arms, but the King forbade them to go any further. "It is for God and Oliver to arrange his maintenance! Let no man come between them."

Their worried eyes fixed again on the terrible scene.

FIERABRAS stood before his helpless foe, his chest heaving and a stern, triumphant look on his face. "Now you *must* surrender. Without a sword you've no more strength than a woman."

"Take me first, then make your boasts."

"I tell you true, Sir Oliver, wounded as you are I have never met your peer. Your death would ill-please me. Let me do this instead. Abandon your God – you must see now that He won't sustain you – and swear your loyalty to Mahon. Do this and I will see you a King in your own right and married to my sister Floripas, than whom there is no fairer maid in all the world."

"Whilst I live I will never yield."

Little remained of Oliver's shield but bent and battered pieces that curled around his arm. What there was, he moved in the path of the giant's cut. The force of the blow threw him ten feet through the air.

Fierabras followed, swinging again. This stroke passed the knight's defense and cut through the circle of his helm. It fell to the ground in two pieces, leaving Oliver bareheaded and bleeding from a gash on the brow.

"This is absurd!" Fierabras cried. "What honor do you gain from dying like this? Your God and your King have abandoned you. Join with me and you'll live with the honor and wealth you deserve."

"The day is not yet done, nor am I abandoned. Your words are naught but a folly."

"Very well," said Fierabras. "Let this be the test of our faiths. He that wins will prove his God the strongest, once and for all."

Fierabras raised his sword and stalked forward again. Oliver rolled away from a downward slash, and Plourance carved a foot-deep trench in the ground. A sweeping, side-to-side blow followed, which forced the knight to retreat, then another, quicker blow as Fierabras reversed his wrist and cut across the same line with a sudden lunge to close the distance.

Unable to back away, Oliver dove to the earth and tumbled desperately between the giant's feet. He leapt up as fast as he could, and found himself eye to eye with the Saracen's huge, black stallion. He blanched, but the horse merely stood – with a look of curiosity on his face and his master's other blades hanging by the saddle. Oliver grasped the larger of the two with both hands and spun to face his attacker.

"Now we shall see the end of this!"

Like a hungry lion, Oliver leapt on his gigantic foe and smote with all his strength. Fierabras' heavy shield cracked in two at the impact and the bottom half went skittering across the grass. The next blow sent the giant's helm flying and left a deep cut that poured stinging blood into his eye.

These strokes made Fierabras sore afraid – all the more, as he knew well the sword's history and lineage – but this was a giant with the soul of a valiant knight. The shadow had barely crossed his eye before a look of hard determination took its place.

Oliver was astonished. *'This is a fierce and noble man,'* he thought, *'even if he is a heathen. If only Charles had him in hand and could bring him to be baptized. Roland and I could be true friends to a knight such as this!'*

Fierabras took the initiative and attacked suddenly, hoping to overwhelm his smaller foe with weight and strength. Oliver was again too quick. He dropped to one knee and thrust upward as the giant's blow passed overhead. The point found a section of Fierabras' armor that had been torn during the day's combat and sank between his ribs. With a strangled cry, the Saracens' mightiest knight collapsed to the earth and curled into a ball.

CHAPTER 8 – CAPTURES AND RESCUES

Fierabras looked up at his conqueror and choked, "The day is yours, noble knight. I cry mercy and acknowledge that your God is the strongest. Take me to your camp, I beg you, so I may be yielded unto Charlemagne before I die."

This speech stirred in Oliver such compassion that his eyes overflowed with tears. "That would please me greatly," he said. "Only the one horse remains. I will ride for help."

"Take me with you, I beg. My death is nigh, and now that I've become Christian I must fear the terrors of hell that await if I die unbaptized or without the final rites."

"I won't leave you," Oliver promised. With great care he helped Fierabras to mount before him. Then he chuckled. "But this horse may leave us both before he manages to carry our doubled weight."

A rumble rose from the west before the stallion could take a single step. Fierabras looked stricken. "That must be my army. I left fifty thousand of my subjects in yonder wood this morning and bade them to wait until I returned from combat. They must have seen me fall, and now they ride to my rescue. You have done enough, Sir Oliver. Leave me here and flee for safety."

Oliver blanched at this information but answered with a firm voice, "Sir King, where we go, we will go together."

They urged Fierabras' stallion to his utmost speed, but never stood a chance. One tired mount carrying two armored knights – and one of them a giant – has never in all of history outraced fifty thousand Arab steeds. The Saracens closed rapidly.

Again, Fierabras urged Oliver to save himself and again the knight refused. Instead, he reined in the horse and gently helped his former enemy down to rest against a stone. Then he pulled on Fierabras' shield, which was in far better shape than his own, grasped Hautclere in his hand and remounted for battle. Crying "God and King Charles!" he spun the stallion about and charged into the oncoming hoard.

It was a charge the Saracens would long regret. Where rode the son of Reyner, no foe survived. His trail was a swath of death. Even courage has its limits, however. Hampered by his wounds and drowned in numbers, Oliver was eventually overwhelmed and captured. King Sortibrant and King Brullant bound his arms while a fierce Moorish champion called Maradas tied a blindfold over his eyes.

Oliver called out for help – to Roland, Thierry and the King himself – but this only made Maradas laugh. "Whoever you are Frenchman, you call in vain. I shall not eat before seeing you hanged in the Admiral's court." He gave the helpless, blindfolded knight a buffet and then laughed again.

THE FRENCH, seeing Oliver's distress, quickly armed and rode out en masse to save him. They could see him being carried off – could hear his cries – but the press was so thick they had to fight for every inch.

Not a man among the French but slew a Saracen that day. Each of the knights slew dozens, at least. As for Roland, he accounted for many score with his hand alone, and hundreds more beside; for the foe held him in such terror that the mere sight of his red and white surcoat set all but the hardiest heathens to their heels where they became easy prey for the rest of the King's army. But all was for naught in the end. Sortibrant and Brullant took Oliver in charge and easily outdistanced the wrathful pursuit, especially when the Saracen reinforcements from Mantryble began to move forward.

Charlemagne cried out to his army, "Would you abandon your friends? Ride! Ride for their lives!" The men answered with a roar and pressed forward with renewed vigor. Roland, ever in front, wielded Durandal like a bolt of silver lightning that stuck down foes by the score. Nevertheless, the sun was low before the Saracen lines finally shattered.

The French vanguard dashed forward, ripping a full five miles through the retreating enemy, but even this proved fruitless. Night fell and the men who'd ridden the furthest were suddenly attacked from ambush. When other captives began to be taken, the grudging King was finally forced to call off the chase.

Charlemagne returned from this disappointment to find the injured Fierabras all but bled out where Oliver had left him. "I have good cause to hate you Pagan," said the King. "You have cost me many good knights this day."

Fierabras bowed his head and said, "Nevertheless, I thank God for your coming. Most noble King, I beg your mercy to let me be baptized so I may die without fear for my soul. If I live, I will do all that I can to advance your cause, and will serve you forever as my liege."

The King's anger drained to compassion when he heard Fierabras speak so humbly. He agreed without demur and called for Bishop Turpin to perform the rite.

So it came to pass that Fierabras, who eventually recovered from his wounds, was baptized as "Florin", though men never ceased to call him by his original name.

In other times, this would have been cause enough for a great celebration – doubly so since the same day had seen a Saracen army routed from the field. On this night, however, not a man of the realm greeted the stars with joy. Oliver was gone and with him four other doughty knights: Geoffrey of Anjou, William the Scot, Duke Basyn of Bordeaux and Gerard of Montdidier, who was the son of Duke Thierry. Five of the Twelve Peers were lost.

THE SARACENS who had taken Oliver and the others rode without pause until they'd passed over the great Mantryble Bridge and come to the Admiral's rich city of Aygremore. There, Sortibrant and Brullant had the prisoners bound in chains and dragged to the Admiral's palace.

Oliver spoke low to the others as they arrived. "Be cautious. Our lives would end in a minute if this Admiral should ever discover we are Peers of France." They nodded understanding.

Balan, the Admiral of Spain, came out upon the terrace. "Sortibrant! Brullant! My good friends. Do you come with tidings of how my son Fierabras has struck off the head of the Emperor Charles and put his Peers to flight?"

"Not exactly, your Excellency. Fierabras was vanquished in single combat by one of the King's knights. We attacked at once, but Roland was there and our army was set to rout. Despite all this, we have captured the man who struck down your son and also four knights of his company."

The Admiral waxed exceedingly wroth as he heard the evil news. His face contorted, grew bright red, and so much spit flew out that he couldn't speak a word. His arms trembled on the terrace rail. "Bring the devil forth!" he finally cried.

Despite his will, Balan found himself impressed at Oliver's fairness of form and noble bearing. "What great Baron of France are you, to bring low the greatest knight in all of Spain?"

"No Baron am I," said Oliver, "nor any man who follows me. We are but poor, bachelor knights who joined the King in hope of booty and fame."

"*What?* I thought I had Peers of France! Five keys, as it were, to the heart of the Court. These are useless. Tie them to a tree and bring me my bow. I will use their bodies for practice."

Sortibrant hurried forward. "Excellency, it is too late to do proper justice now. Let us wait until tomorrow, when you can think of some more appropriate way to dispose of the captives."

"Very well. Send them to the Pit."

THE FIVE captive knights were straight away taken and cast into the pit that served as the Admiral's dungeon. This was a hideous place that nourished toads, rats, insects and serpents of all kinds. Worse, it filled with seawater as the tide rose, which would have drowned the captives but for two fifteen-foot tall pillars on which they could climb for safety.

Oliver suffered from this greatly. The fatigue of the day's battle had settled on him and the saltwater made his wounds smart beyond bearing. Had it not been for Gerard of Montdidier, who supported him on the stone, he would surely have drowned. Even so, the pain was such that he could neither hear nor speak, and his fellow knights were consumed with worry that he would perish there before them.

Oliver was in no condition to remember it, but Fierabras had mentioned a sister. Up in her chamber, Floripas could hear both the Admiral's laments and the cries of the captives beneath. Moved with pity, she went to the hall with twelve of her ladies to discover the cause. On hearing that her brother had been vanquished and taken prisoner her moans outstripped all the rest. But after a time her grief softened. She went, alone, to the jailer and asked the identity of the men whose suffering could be heard so clear.

"My lady, they are men from the army of Charles, the very same who vanquished your brother Fierabras. One, though sore injured, is as comely a knight as I have ever seen. They say it was he who did the evil deed."

"Open the door. I wish to see them."

"My lady, you must not. It is too evil a place for gentle eyes, filled as it is with snakes, toads and vermin of all sorts. Moreover, your father the Admiral has commanded that no one may lay eyes on the captives until morning, and most especially not a woman. *'Always remember,'* he told me, *'that women are changeable, inconstant, and not to be trusted in such affairs, and bear in mind how many men have been led astray by their doings.'* I can not let you pass."

Floripas paled with rage. "You beast! How dare you speak such words to me!"

She wrenched the heavy keys from his belt and beat them on his head until only a corpse lay in her path. "Not to be trusted... *Hmmph!*" Then she opened the door and called down into the pit.

"WHO ARE YOU that defeated my brother, the mighty Fierabras?"

The knights, though amazed to hear a gentle voice, responded politely. "We are knights of France, good lady, cast into this hideous dungeon by the Admiral of Spain. Would that we could only die cleanly in battle instead of lingering in this horrible place!"

Floripas could be moved by courteous speech even though she was a heathen. Her heart softened. "It may be that I can provide you with that chance. But first you must promise to aid me in gaining my desire."

"Lady," they said quickly, "if you free us and arm us we will serve you however we may."

"Then come," she said.

Floripas let down a rope so the knights might climb to the door where she stood, then motioned them to follow her silently by a secret way up to her rooms. "Do you know a knight of your land named Guy of Burgundy?" she whispered to Oliver, the knight who was nearest by.

"Indeed I do," he answered, "as fine a gentleman as any in the realm. He is a cousin of Roland and was newly made a companion of the King's high table."

"Know then that I have loved him since the first moment I saw him over the battlements of Rome. We have never met but he holds my heart more surely than anyone else ever could."

"You may rest assured, good lady," said Oliver. "If ever we make our way to Guy, I will plead your suit with all the powers at my command."

AT ABOUT this time the group finally arrived at Floripas' chambers. The Admiral's stronghold was a mighty tower five hundred feet high, which stood on a rise outside of the city. The rear of the tower edged up against a sheer cliff that overlooked the sea, while a broad moat, spanned by a single, heavily fortified, solid iron drawbridge, made the front equally impregnable. Several private alcoves extended from the tower, including one especially fair and gracious suite that belonged to Floripas. It was to this private haven that she took the five knights.

Floripas' maid, Maragonde, met her Lady and the knights as they entered her chamber. She took one look at the knights and began to tremble. "My lady!" she whispered anxiously. "Do you know who stands there beside you? I recognize them. The fair one is Oliver, Roland's friend. Beside him is Gerard of Montdidier, and William the Scot, and.... My lady, I must find your father the Admiral and tell him of this! No doubt he'll give me a great reward!"

"Indeed?" said Floripas. "I had no idea. You must tell him with all speed. But wait – I hear my father through yon window. We can call down to him from there."

Maragonde hurried to the window and looked out. "My lady, it is too dark. I can't see him."

"You just need to look closer," said Floripas. She put a soft hand on Maragonde's shoulder and pushed. The traitorous maid flew out the window and down to the sea. "There. Now you have the reward you deserve."

From that day on, Floripas hid the five knights in a secret room. She let it out that they'd been drowned and dragged off by the beasts of the pit, a rumor which people readily accepted. It had happened before, and besides: since escape was impossible, there could be no other answer. The jailer's body went swimming with the maid's. No one ever noticed or wondered where either one had gone.

CHARLEMAGNE had not rested idle with so many good knights taken captive. As Duke Reyner poured out tears for his missing son, the King paced back and forth in his tent, furious at the loss of the others almost as much as Oliver. Finally he turned to Roland.

"Good nephew. I pray thee: mount thy horse and take a message for me to Admiral Balan. Tell him that if he does not return my knights, swear fealty for his lands, abandon his false gods and consent to be baptized, I shall come to him at Aygremore and there hang him by his neck before all his people."

"Sire, you must reconsider!" said Roland. "If I deliver such a message you will never see me again."

"You will do as I command this time or I will hang you myself! Naymon, what do you think of this?"

"That if you command him to bring such a message you will never see him alive again."

"Then you can go with him. Ogier, what is your opinion?"

"The same as Duke Naymon's."

"That makes three."

So it went until seven of the Peers were chosen: Count Roland, Duke Naymon, Ogier the Dane, Duke Richard of Normandy, Duke Thierry of Ardennes, Aubrey of Bordeaux, who was the son of the captured Duke Basyn, and Roland's younger cousin, Guy of Burgundy. The knights confessed themselves as men going to death and then rode off to the general lamentation of the army. A sudden fear struck the King as he watched them pass to the West, but his word had been given and his word could not be changed.

"There's nothing to do now but put your faith in God," said Ganelon, his glee well hidden. No less worried than the King, Bishop Turpin could do nothing but agree with those words; albeit sincerely.

EARLIER THAT DAY the Admiral had likewise determined to rescue his son, Fierabras, and had summoned a force of twenty kings and princes to bear his terms to Charles. Brullant and Maradas, the great Moorish champion, were to lead the party.

"What message shall we deliver?" asked Brullant.

"Tell Charles that if he does not return my son, swear fealty for his lands, abandon his God and swear to serve Mahon, I shall come to him at Paris and there hang him by his neck before all his people."

Brullant was not well pleased to carry such a message, and Sortibrant supported him. "Sire, this is an ill-thought plan. You should listen to Brullant. He and I are like old dogs. If you stick by the tail of an old dog you'll never go astray."

The Admiral scowled, "Do you question me?"

Doubt as they might, none of the kings or princes would meet his ruler's eye, so all twenty rode out soon after. They crossed the River

Flagot late that morning at Mantryble, and continued on their way toward the enemy camp. Halfway there, a group of seven French knights rode into view from the opposite direction. The Heathens didn't know it but these were the very knights bearing the message of Charles.

Maradas reined up short. "If I'm to be civil to a Christian king, I must first slake my thirst for Christian blood," he declared. There being general agreement to this sentiment, the Saracen party halted. The others watched in good cheer as their hero rode forth and began to call insults at the approaching French.

Roland had never dealt well with insults. When he understood the Saracen's words, his famous sword Durandal leapt to his hand with the speed of thought and he spurred his horse rose smoothly to a run.

It must be said that Maradas was a very great champion of the heathen folk and the victor in more than two hundred duels. His hand was so heavy that more than a few doughty soldiers swore oaths by his strength. The stroke he laid upon Roland shocked the French knight with its power. It even drove down the corner of his shield. Roland answered, however, with a blow that snaked around Maradas' guard like a living thing. Durandal crushed the Saracen's helmet like cloth and hurled him to the ground in a heap of scattered brains.

The Heathen kings roared in shock and dismay, and charged at the smaller group of French. This was no ordinary band, however, and for once the Saracens had laid no ambush. The knights tore through them like a scythe. Before long, all the Saracen Kings but Brullant lay dead on the field, and he was flying with all his speed for Aygremore.

The Peers rested for a while, then Duke Naymon stood to address the company. "My lords, I counsel that we return now to Charles and tell him what we have done. I've no doubt that a triumph such as this will content him well, and he shall release us from this madness upon which we've been sent."

"How can you speak of returning?" demanded Roland, leaping to his feet. "So long as Durandal hangs by my side and I have a hand to hold her, I'll have no thought but to deliver this message to Admiral Balan, damned be he and all his kind! No, let us do this instead. Let us each take one of these Saracen heads and present them to the Admiral as our gift."

"Sir Roland, you must be out of your wits!" said Naymon. "If we do as you counsel, the Admiral would have us slain before the message could even be given."

Thierry and the others agreed with Roland, however, so it ended with each man taking up a head and riding forth on their way. Before long they came to the town of Mantryble. This town lay on one of the mightiest torrents in the world: the Flagot, a river so wide, deep and fast that a man caught in its waters would fly downstream faster than a bolt from a crossbow. The only way across for days in any direction was the great Mantryble Bridge, about which Ogier the Dane had a frightening intelligence.

"The bridge is wide enough for twenty knights to ride abreast, and is built on thirty great arches of marble. All are strong, well spaced, broad, and equipped with bars of iron that may be dropped at need. The road is sealed with cement and lead, and at either end is a great drawbridge that may be raised with ten heavy iron chains. The drawbridge works are housed in towers of marvelous strength, each forty feet tall and topped with a resplendent gold eagle that glows like a flame. Finally, the warden of the bridge is a huge giant, as fierce as any I've ever seen. Men say his name is Galafer and he bears a man-sized, steel-headed axe to destroy those who oppose his will."

The messengers were much dismayed at this news and would have turned back but for Roland. "Never fear, my friends," he said. "With Durandal in my hand I value no pagan ever born at more than a penny, whatsoever his size may be."

Duke Naymon disagreed. "Sir Roland, it helps us not at all to give one stroke and then receive a hundred. Let me take care of this and, God willing, we will pass by without danger."

This displeased Roland but the others agreed to the plan. The group rode on with its white bearded elder in the lead.

GALAFER, warden of the Mantryble Bridge, was even larger than Fierabras though far less noble in appearance, thought and deed. Backed by a hundred soldiers armed with heavy glaives, he stopped the company before they could even set foot on the bridge.

"Whither go you, old man, and on what business?" he thundered down at Duke Naymon.

"Giant, we are heralds of King Charles who bear a message to the Admiral Balan. More, your Admiral owes us a service, for just this morning we came across twenty villains on the road that would have done us ill. We've brought you their heads to dispose of properly to your dogs."

With that, Naymon and the others tossed the heads of seven Saracen kings to the ground.

Galafer recognized the dead faces rolling around his feet and went almost out of his wits with anger. "Understand me vassal," he boomed at Duke Naymon. "You will go nowhere unless you pay my bridge toll first."

"Demand what ye ought to have, Porter, and we will content you."

"It is no light toll. You must pay me thirty couples of hounds trained to the hunt; one hundred maidens, chaste and of good manners; one hundred falcons ready to fly; one hundred steeds trained for war; and for every wing and foot, a mark of gold with horses and wagons to carry it. Only then may you pass. Fail to make this payment and you will die where you stand."

Naymon waved a hand and said, "Is that all you require? If so, you shall be content before midday tomorrow. Our baggage comes closely behind us with more than a hundred thousand laden horses, maidens as fair as any, and hawks and hounds in great abundance. Too, there are hauberks, helms and shields without number. Take of them such as shall please you."

So saying, Naymon led the other knights out and over the bridge. Galafer stepped aside. In truth, he was so occupied with counting his forthcoming treasure that he barely saw them pass.

"Truly, Sir Duke," said Roland, "your strategy is proven. By your words we have passed this bridge without danger."

A lone Saracen came by as he spoke, headed the other way. Without hesitation Roland stepped down from his horse, picked the man up and hurled him over the side of the bridge into the torrential River Flagot. "Praise God," he said. "Now all things have turned out well indeed."

Naymon saw the pagan fall and flushed with anger. He muttered through tight lips, "Lord God of Heaven, guard us well. This Count has no patience, and I fear his temper shall one day lead us all to a villainous death! At least we're rid of those damned heads."

The company rode on past Mantryble and then settled down to sleep in a clearing off the road.

BY RIDING hard through the night, Brullant managed to arrive at the Admiral's city of Aygremore just as his lord rose from the morning meal. "What are you doing here?" cried the Admiral from his terrace. "Where are Maradas and the others?"

"Slain, one and all," said Brullant. "We came across a troop of seven Frenchmen who killed everyone but me. I barely escaped with my life to bring you this news."

Balan trembled at the tidings, and then began to turn colors, stutter, and drool. He finally grew so wroth that he turned on one of the guards and threw him over a railing into the moat, cursing the man the whole way down.

When his liege had at last calmed down, Sortibrant stepped up and laid a hand across Brullant's shoulders. "Next time, your Majesty, you would do better to heed our counsel. Stick close to the tail of an old dog and you'll never go astray."

With tears in his eyes, the Admiral bowed his head and nodded.

THE SEVEN Peers arrived that afternoon and immediately demanded an audience with the Admiral to deliver their message. Brullant leaned over the Admiral's shoulder and whispered, "These are the men who slew your Kings and Princes! Guard them well."

Sortibrant added, "Yes. Guard them well, but first let us hear what the French King has to say."

Nodding, Admiral Balan stood to greet the embassy.

Duke Naymon put an arm across Roland's chest. "I will speak first. Your tongue would have us all dead before the rest of us could say a word."

Though ill content, Roland bowed his head in agreement. Naymon stepped forward and spoke in a clear, strong voice.

"God keep the noble King Charlemagne, puissant, strong and wise Emperor, as well as Roland, Oliver, and the other peers of France; and confound, from the top of the head to the bottom of the feet, the Admiral here present, inasmuch as his subjects were just yesterday on a mission of evil purpose beyond the Mantryble Bridge. We found twenty scoundrels on the field who would have taken our horses. God be thanked, they paid for this a heavy price."

The Admiral began to rage when he understood this speech. His face turned red, then white, and then red again. Foam formed at his lips. Brullant, who had been the one to escape the day before, calmed him from acting too rashly. "Let us discover their errand before delivering judgment."

The Admiral nodded. "Continue your message," he said to Naymon.

"The great and noble King of France commands that you abandon your false gods, consent to be baptized, swear fealty for your lands, render to him the stolen treasures and relics from Rome, and deliver up his knights whom you now hold in prison. If you fail to do as I have described, Charles shall cause you to be hanged by the neck on a gibbet and strangled villainously before your people."

The Admiral answered, "You have greatly defiled me with this outrage, but I have listened patiently. Go and stand by yonder pillar until I have heard these others. May my god Mahon give me an evil death if I either eat or drink until I see your head separated from your shoulders."

The next knight repeated the message as Duke Naymon had given it. "You remind me of Richard of Normandy," said the Admiral. "The man who slew my uncle Corsuble. Would that Richard was indeed here. He would die an even quicker death than the rest of you. Go and stand by your ancient friend."

Ogier delivered the message proudly in a deep, booming voice, as was his wont. After him came Guy of Burgundy, Aubrey of Bordeaux and Duke Thierry, whose visage was so fierce and awful that the Admiral recoiled and made gestures as one might against a demon. All spoke just as Naymon had until Roland. He came last and added, "But as for me, I care little whether you obey this command or not, for I count you lower than the carcass of a dog that lies rotting in the summer sun."

At this the Admiral's eyes almost popped from his head, but he choked down his rage and turned to Sortibrant and Brullant. "Very well, then. What do you advise?"

Sortibrant said, "Sire, let these miscreants be cut to pieces here before our eyes."

Brullant added, "And then take an army to conquer this Charles from whom these words came first."

The Admiral liked both of these suggestions, but before he could act his daughter arrived at his side.

CHAPTER 9 – THE TOWER

Floripas looked at the company of knights and asked, "Father, who are these men?"

"They are knights of King Charles who have reproached me with uncivil words and demands. What do you recommend I do with them, dear?"

"Smite off their heads and burn their bodies outside the city. But let it wait until after dinner. One cannot enjoy justice on an empty stomach. I will take charge of the prisoners until then."

"An excellent idea, daughter!"

Sortibrant tried to intervene. "Sire, you should not entrust so heavy a task to a woman. They are changeable, inconstant and not to be trusted in such affairs. Think of how many men have been led astray by the doings of women."

"Nonsense. This is my daughter. She's different.

"See they are guarded well, Floripas." The Admiral went to eat, motioning for his subject kings to follow.

Floripas watched her father leave in one direction, then turned on her heel and motioned for the captives to follow her in another. As she led them to her rooms Duke Naymon sighed quietly to Roland, "If it's a captive I'm to be, God be thanked for giving me such a jailer. Did you ever see a maiden more fair?"

"This is not the time to dwell on such things," Roland answered curtly.

"I, too, was once young," said the Duke.

"Hush," said Floripas. "This is no time to argue amongst yourselves."

They traveled the rest of the way in silence. When the last man had entered, Floripas bolted the door behind him and straightaway moved across the room where, without a word, she opened the secret chamber that sheltered Oliver and the other men she had rescued.

The knights within and without crowded the threshold, weeping with joy at their reunion. None were happier than Roland and Oliver, who clasped each other with frank and tender hearts, each demanding to hear of the other's adventures since they were parted.

Floripas waited a generous time before speaking. "My lords, since I have done you this service, will you now undertake to help me gain my desire?"

"Most willingly, fair one," said Duke Naymon. "Name your wish and you may trust in our faith."

"You speak most politely, reverend sir. May I know your name and state?"

"I am called Naymon, Duke of Bavaria and messenger of His Majesty, King Charles of France."

Floripas was much astonished at her guest's illustrious rank and dipped a graceful curtsey. Then she asked after the names of his comrades. The first man Naymon introduced was Richard of Normandy, from whom Floripas recoiled in shock. "It was you who slew my uncle Corsuble outside the gates of Rome! I should hate you for that, but for the love of these others will grant you my pardon."

Then Naymon introduced her to Roland. On hearing this name, Floripas gave a little cry and fell to her knees. "Blessed sir, I love a certain knight, a cousin of yours named Guy of Burgundy. It is to have him for husband that I have risked all this. Have you any tidings of him you could share?"

"My news is old," said Roland. "Why not ask him yourself? Not four feet of space lies between you. Guy! Come forward and greet your bride."

Guy blanched. "God forbid I should marry any woman but one given by the King's own hand!"

Floripas paled. Her eyes and face grew still, and her voice turned strangely flat. "Say not so, or I swear by Mahon that all the knights in this room will be hanged by morning."

Oliver and the other knights who had been captive for a longer time made frantic shushing motions to Guy from behind Floripas' back. *"For God's sake man...!"* Oliver urged in a harsh whisper.

Even Roland began to look distinctly uncomfortable. "Greet her with joy Guy, and give the lady what she desires."

Guy paused a moment, then rolled his eyes and said, "Oh, very well."

Floripas gave a little squeal of joy and leapt to embrace him. She held him close but did not kiss him, being still unbaptized. When they parted, Guy looked more than a little bemused but also less upset. Women like Floripas will have that effect.

BACK AT the main hall, the Admiral had just sat down to eat when King Iblis of Samarkand stepped up to the table. "Greetings, my lord. Where is your daughter this evening, she who is my promised bride?"

"She has carried to prison some captives who came bearing an evil message from Charles."

"Sire, you do a great folly to trust such tasks to a woman. They are changeable, inconstant, and not to be trusted in such affairs. Just think of how many men have been led astray by the doings of women! Let me go and make sure that all is well."

"You have Our permission to leave, but return soon and bring Our daughter to join us at table."

Iblis hurried to Floripas' chamber and pressed his ear to the door. Hearing the murmur of voices within, he stepped back, raised his foot, and smote the door so strongly that the bolts broke apart and it flew from its hinges.

Outrage flashed over Floripas' face as he strode in past the wreckage. She leaned over to whisper in Roland's ear, "I am ill content at this violence against me. This man insists he will be my husband, but I'd rather be gnawed to death by snakes. I love Guy and no one else. Prithee – avenge me for this dishonor."

Roland smiled. "Doubt it not Mademoiselle. Ere he departs that man will know he has done an evil deed. No one ever paid more for the buying of a lock than he shall pay for the breaking of yours."

Iblis surveyed the crowded room and then marched over to Duke Naymon, whom he grasped by the long, white beard. "Who are you old man, and why have you come? Tell me the truth!"

"I would not lie to such as you. I am Naymon of Bavaria, and I come here as a messenger of Charles, my King, that your Admiral might know what must be done to avoid his certain destruction. Now take your hand from my beard and be sure I do not say all I'd like."

"Bah," said Iblis, throwing down the beard and almost Naymon with it. "I would be content if the Admiral pardoned your folly, but I need to know more for my own plans. By your loyalty, tell me: what manner of men are these French and their King? What is their enterprise and what do they do for games?"

With growing ire, Duke Naymon answered, "The French are of all types, like other men, and after the King has dined they go about their diverse affairs. Some ride, some hunt, some hawk. Some sing, some dance, some regale with stories and tales. Some play at chess. Others go to mass. But when they go to battle they are fierce and hardy, one and all. Such are the folk of France."

"These are but follies," said Iblis. "How do they do at blowing the great coal?"

Duke Naymon eyed him suspiciously. "Blowing the great coal? I do not know the game. Moreover..." He broke off when he saw Roland making little signals to abide the man a bit longer. Another of the knights edged over to the broken door.

"Then I will show you!" said Iblis, who'd missed the byplay. He strode to the fire at the center of the room and selected the heaviest brand. "See you this?" He held the burning wood up toward Duke Naymon. "Watch carefully."

When the Duke leaned in he blew on the coal sharply, so that sparks flew up and into Naymon's eye. Iblis roared with laughter. "Now you try."

Naymon took the brand and blew on it so fiercely that flames bellowed forth and set the heathen's beard on fire. Iblis screeched with rage and reached for his sword, but Naymon took the torch and struck the evil man so great a blow that his neck broke and his eyes popped out to roll on the floor.

"False creature. You sought to amuse yourself on me? Lie there, then, in sorrow."

"In truth, your Grace," said Roland, "you play most excellently at the great coal."

"Judge me not, my lords," said Naymon. "You saw how he trifled with me."

Floripas touched his arm lightly. "We will judge you naught but kindly, for Iblis had no leave to be playing at the coal with you. Now he is at peace and so am I, for never more shall he seek to force me into marriage. I would rather have had my hands smitten off or died a villainous death."

THE LADY turned her gaze to include the entire company. "There is no help for it now. My father will be awaiting Iblis' return with great eagerness. You must arm yourselves and conquer the Tower. Slay all within; you have no friends here but my ladies and me.

"Do brave deeds, my Guy," she added quietly.

The knights cleared the upper rooms quickly, then burst in to the main part of the tower, slaying as they went. The Admiral and his nobles were surprised at their meat and had no chance. All but a very few died where they sat. One who escaped, however, was the Admiral himself.

Roland spied him at the head of the table and bolted across the room. Six guards – well-armed knights of Balan's house – leapt in Roland's way. This was an uneven match, but they managed to delay him just long enough for the Admiral to leap out a window. Even so it was close. Durandal sank a foot deep into the marble stone of the windowsill, and missed her target by no more than a hair.

"I see you lost one," said Oliver to his friend.

"Aye," Roland answered, "the worst rat in all the nest. I fear we shall pay for this."

They turned as one to finish the work together.

SPUTTERING, soaked and looking like a rat indeed, the Admiral was helped from the moat by Sortibrant and Brullant, who'd left earlier to see about raising the gibbet. "Your daughter must have betrayed us, Sire," said Sortibrant. "Did I not warn you that she couldn't be trusted?"

"Never mind that now. Gather my army and call my vassals. We will take back the Tower at dawn and deal with all of the criminals then, whatever their sex."

The French finished securing the gate and drawbridge, then paused to take stock of their situation. The fortress was well provisioned with a cistern of water but had no larder to speak of. With twelve knights,

Floripas, and twenty of her ladies to feed, the supplies would last for no more than three days.

Ogier the Dane shook his head. "This is grim news. They need only be patient and our position will soon be hopeless. We must be bold to survive."

"Do not worry," said Floripas, "if the gods favor our cause we shall not want."

The lady could afford such optimism, of course, because she knew the virtue of her magic girdle; that all who looked upon her would be satisfied as if they'd been at a feast. This secret she kept to herself, however, seeing no reason to share it.

Unfortunately, the Admiral already knew.

THE HEATHEN, as all men know, are as famous for their thieving ways as they are for their love of drink. But in Aygremore there lived a certain thief named Mervyn who was more skilled than any other. It was said he could steal the moon herself and the night would never know. The Admiral sent for this Mervyn and gave him the task of stealing Floripas' magic girdle. "Do this," he said, "and I'll pardon your crimes and fill your pockets with silver coin."

Mervyn agreed with the long, low bow of an experienced courtier. When night fell most deeply, he climbed the sheer Tower wall and slipped through a high window into the lady's sleeping chamber. A magic charm he possessed ensured that everyone would be asleep. Sliding carefully to Floripas' sleeping form, he unlaced the magic girdle and tied it around his own waist.

At that point Mervyn the thief should have left – and knew he should have left – but instead he paused to gaze on the slumbering maiden. So beautiful... and so alone... his passion overwhelmed him and he lay down to ravish her.

Floripas woke as the thief's weight fell upon her. Freed from the spell, she bit the hand on her mouth and then screamed. Mervyn leapt to his feet and ran for the open window, but found it was already too late.

Guy of Burgundy had been sleeping just outside the door and charged inside at the maiden's cry. With a single, smooth motion, he drew his sword, and sliced the rascal in half. Then he knelt at Floripas' side.

She clung to him, weeping hysterically at what had nearly happened. When the other knights arrived, they left the pair alone and silently gathered the pieces of Mervyn's body. These were hurled down to the moat.

It took almost an hour before Floripas calmed down enough to realize that her magic girdle was missing. At that point she screamed again, but to less avail. Cut in half along with the thief, the girdle lay in two pieces down in the sea.

The Admiral and Sortibrant, on watch outside the Tower, heard Floripas' wail. "The thief does not return, Sire," said Sortibrant. "He must have failed in his mission."

"Perhaps. Time will tell. But either way, we attack in the morning."

THE SARACEN army poured toward the Tower but soon found that the moat and other defenses were so strong that only a few hundred attackers could press forward at once. That was not enough. A storm of darts from the sturdy French crushed the morning assault.

The Admiral drove a second wave over the bodies of the first, and when the second failed, a third. They had even less success. The only result was a new wall of corpses that reinforced the defense.

When night fell and foreclosed any further attacks, the French laughed and jeered from the high windows. Admiral Balan ground his teeth. "We will starve them out instead," he said.

This, it turned out, was an excellent plan.

Four days of siege exhausted the Tower's food supply so thoroughly that the defenders were forced to scavenge among the vermin that lived in the Admiral's dungeon. The ladies, unused to such hardship, suffered profoundly. Finally even Floripas fainted from want.

She came to herself in Guy's arms and began to lament. "Now it is proved that you should worship my Gods. Your Jesus on his cross has done nothing to help us, but Mahon and Margotte would surely give us food and wine for succor."

These words angered many of the knights but Guy waved them to silence. "Take us to your Gods," he said, "and we will see what may be."

Floripas led them to a high, locked room, took a silver key from her bodice and opened the heavy door. The men froze utterly still.

"My God!" gasped Gerard of Montdidier. "With that much gold the King could raise a cathedral for every church the Admiral has burned." Even Duke Naymon, who had seen many treasures in his long life, and Duke Basyn, who ruled the rich fief of Bordeaux, had never seen a more fabulous display. Overflowing chests of coins and gems covered the floor, sometimes piled higher than a man's head. Layer on layer of gold bars lined all but one of the walls. The air smelled of myrrh.

The final wall held idols to the many heathen Gods. At the center was Mahon, twice the size of a man and made of solid gold with jewels for eyes and a diamond navel. Next to him sat Apollo and Termagant, each cast in silver with eyes of beryl. Beyond these were seven other idols, all intricately carved and draped with necklaces and strands of precious pearl.

Floripas bent her knee and bowed her head. "Come pray with me and these will give us all the food we need."

"Lady, I cannot," said Ogier the Dane, "for I perceive that your gods are powerless and asleep."

He strode forward and with a single, mighty heave threw down the idol of Mahon. It cracked in two, and an eye went skittering across the floor. Gerard of Montdidier followed right behind and treated the statue of Apollo to a similar fate.

Floripas collapsed in a faint. Guy dropped to her side and gently chaffed her hand. "Good lady, are you well?" Her eyes fluttered slowly open.

"You live," she said with astonished delight. "My Guy, you still live!" Looking around, she added, "And so do the others. Oh Guy, my love, forgive my lack of faith. I had doubts before, but after this day I will never again believe in Mahon or any other God but the one we share together."

Duke Naymon reproved her gently. "Nay, good lady. Your confusion is easy to understand. You were taught to worship these idols as a child, to whom words of adults seem little less than those of another sort of god. And just as adults will sometimes deceive a child in order to control her, so will priests of all sorts deceive their flock in order to gain power, control, or station they could not earn by their birth or virtues alone. Many a rogue has seen the cloth as his path to mischief and wealth! Therefore look you here instead of toward your broken idols."

So saying he reached inside the reliquary that held the treasures stolen from Rome. His hand came out with a single, bent nail. He held this up before her eyes and then released it. The nail did not drop.

"Bishop Turpin has taught us that only one test may be used to tell a true relic from all the frauds that men will claim for whatever wicked reason may drive them that day. But it is an infallible test. A thing that has been touched by the hand of God partakes in equal halves of the earthly and the divine. Release it – thus – and it will not turn toward either state, but rather will hover in between.

"It is by such proofs we can be sure of the One True Faith. Without them we would all be as vulnerable to lies and deceit as you were on the day you first were brought to bend your knee before such as these." He gestured toward the shattered figure of Margotte.

Floripas took the nail from the air, replaced it in its box, and then kissed her fingers gently. "Your Grace, even in Spain you are known as one of the wisest men on earth. Now I know it to be true."

HAPPY AS the knights were to see Floripas' new devotion, there still remained the problem of supplies. They collected in the main hall to discuss the matter.

"As for me," said Ogier, "I would rather die fighting than wither away here for lack of food. And truly, the lamentations of these maidens turns in my heart more sharp than a dagger."

Oliver voiced his immediate agreement, as did Duke Thierry, Duke Richard and most of the others. After a moment's thought, Duke Naymon joined too. Only Guy of Burgundy remained silent, for his opinion was clear already.

"Very well then," said Oliver. "It is decided. Let us sally forth and obtain some victualing or die in the attempt."

The knights donned their arms and armor, and then gathered by the Tower gate. "Someone must stay and guard the way," said Roland. "You, Sir Naymon, and you, Sir Ogier; I pray thee to abide here that the rest of us may be sure of a safe return. "

Naymon answered angrily. "Sir Roland, do you think me so slight of limb and lineage that I should be your porter? It will not do. I may be old, but I'm yet hard enough of sinew and bone to smite whomsoever I strike."

"Sir, you say well and may join us. Thierry, Geoffrey; let you abide instead."

They liked the task no more than Duke Naymon but bowed to Roland's wish and agreed to stand guard over the safety of the Tower and the ladies inside. Together, the pair raised the portcullis and lowered the drawbridge, then watched as the others charged outside and overwhelmed the besieging guards.

Admiral Balan saw the knights' sally and swiftly sent for Brullant, Sortibrant and his other advisors. "My kings and counselors, behold: the French have taken the field. I shall be ill content with you if any of them live when the sun has set. Assemble your people and ride!"

A great multitude poured from the city but Roland, with Durandal in his hand and his fellows at his side, swept down upon them like the reaper's scythe. The Peers attacked with such fury that five hundred Saracens were slain in a space of minutes, and unhappy was he who came to succor the rest. The momentum began to change, however, when King Clarion arrived with fifteen thousand men at his back and his dread champion, Rampyr, by his side.

In all of Spain there were no two knights more doughty or feared. Their presence returned some heart to the other Saracens, who began to push in on the French. Rampyr, standing tall in his saddle, was a beacon of order. Bellowing clear and loud, he collected the fragmented units together and soon had organized a proper charge.

This effort split the French party into three pieces. Basyn, Aubrey and Guy were wedged off to one part of the field. Oliver, Duke Richard and Duke Naymon found themselves at another. Unfortunately for the Saracens, the charge also brought Rampyr a few steps too close to the four that managed to hold firm.

"Noble knights, to me!" called Roland. "There is one before us who bars our quest."

Durandal flashed once, then twice again, and a path opened up toward the Saracen lord.

Rampyr met the charging knight with a powerful blow, but he might as well have struck at a thundering storm for Roland's blood was up. His answering stroke sent the heathen's head winging up to the sky. The Saracen army dissolved into a terrified mob as each man fled from this devil and his glittering sword.

The battle continued for some hours after that, waning and waxing, until evening fell and darkness forced a halt to the fighting. Then fortune had her laugh. At one end of the field Gerard of Montdidier cried out, "A train!"

Passing right before the Tower gate were twenty pack horses laden with bread and other supplies. Two guards for every horse rode close by, but that slowed the Peers not at all. Crying for Thierry and Geoffrey to open the gate, Gerard, Ogier, and William the Scot drove the animals in, while Roland, Oliver, and Duke Richard held back those Saracens who sought to interfere.

On the other side of the field, however, Duke Basyn collapsed suddenly when a dart flew out of the night and pierced him in the eye. His son Aubrey fell to his knees over the body, weeping, and soon he too was slain as twenty men leapt on him from all directions. This left only Guy of Burgundy to face King Clarion and the whole of his army. Raising his sword and crying defiance, the young knight spurred toward the foe. His courage was not enough. The Saracens slew his horse halfway there and quickly overwhelmed him beneath dozens of fighting men.

Clarion scoffed at the Frenchman's struggles and had him bound with his hands behind his back and a blindfold over his eyes. Guy called on his comrades, God, and Charlemagne for aid. The heathen king stoppered his cries with a gauntlet to the face.

"Your braying won't help you now. Nor shall your King or your hanging God. You're going alive to the Admiral of Spain whether you will it or not. You'd spend your time better by praying for a swift death than for succor and aid; though neither is very likely, to be sure."

With a wicked laugh he drove Guy in to Aygremore.

CLARION brought Guy to where the Admiral sat in state with a great number of soldiers. The prisoner's appearance had changed mightily since their last meeting, for he'd not eaten in three days and Clarion's men had none-too-gently despoiled him of his arms. But bruised, bloody and dressed in rags though he was, Guy still stood proudly.

"Who are you?" the Admiral demanded. "Tell me the truth and I will see you well treated; lie to me and I'll see you suffer."

"I would never lie to such as you. I am Guy of Burgundy, loyal subject of King Charlemagne and cousin to Roland the Valiant."

"Well do I know your name, and often have I cursed it! For these past many months my daughter has been enamored of you. Now I know to what I can blame these many misfortunes. I will have you torn asunder, be sure. Who are your companions in the Tower?"

"Gladly will I tell you that!" Guy listed their names, ending with Duke Basyn and his son Aubrey, "whom you have slain, but for whose lives, by the grace of God, Charlemagne will charge you dear."

At that point one of the guards could stand Guy's manner no longer. He smote the knight in the face so hard that the blood ran freely down. This set the young knight afire with rage. He burst his leather bonds, grasped the guard by the hair and dealt the man such a blow on the neck that he instantly fell dead. The other guards leapt on Guy like a pack of wolves, tearing with their nails and kicking with their hard boots. Soon he lay still and unconscious. They would have killed him in that way had Balan not intervened.

"I don't want him dead. Not yet. And not so quickly." He motioned curtly for his counselors to join him in chambers.

"My friends," he said when they'd all been seated, "I pray that you advise me how best to dispose of this villain."

Brullant stood first. "Let us erect a gallows near the moat, where the French will readily see it. They will undoubtedly ride to rescue their friend; but knowing this, we will conceal five thousand Turks nearby to spring out and take them captive. Then we may dispose of them all – and of your daughter – at your whim and leisure."

"Moreover," said King Sortibrant, rising to stand by his friend, "if they do not ride forth, what better fate and message could we hope to deliver?"

The council agreed unanimously and the Admiral nodded. "So it will be."

THE NEXT morning a group of ten soldiers rode close to the Tower and built a gallows tree that hung over the moat. The knights gathered, wondering what it could mean. "There can be only one answer," said Duke Naymon. "They mean to hang young Guy before our eyes."

Floripas collapsed in a faint. The knights had just roused her when they heard the desperate voice of Guy himself coming from out the window.

The young knight knew nothing of the Admiral's trap, of course. He'd been beaten unconscious, bound with his hands behind his back, and blinded with a hood tied close about his head. His captors, thirty men with staves, prodded him toward the gallows with cruel jabs and blows to his back and calves. Guy, knowing himself led to his death or worse, cried out in the most pitiful tones to God, Charlemagne and his cousin Roland for aid.

Floripas went to her knees before Roland. "Please," she begged, "rescue my Guy lest my heart be lost forever."

It was a plea they could not resist. Their minds as one, the knights sped wordlessly to their horses and girded on weapons and shields. Roland broke the strange silence as Floripas ran to the drawbridge wheel.

"Lords, now do we place our lives and deaths on so perilous a scale that if any man fails of loyalty or discipline, all will be doomed together. We are but nine and the enemy are beyond count. By the honor of God I therefore pray you to hold together and take heed of each other as best we may, for if we be divided we shall all be hanged. If one man falls let all the rest guard him until he may be remounted – do not leave him for life or death. Do this, and by my life, for so long as I can bear my great sword Durandal you shall have in me a good defender and warrant!"

The knights agreed. They sallied forth with grim expressions as Floripas and her damsels lowered the drawbridge and cheered for them to be valiant and brave.

THE PEERS rode steadily around the Tower toward the gallows where the guards continued to jab and abuse young Guy with staves. His hands were bound behind him and a blindfold covered his eyes. A rope encircled his neck.

Roland spurred his horse and cried out in a fury, "Varlets! What you have begun you will sore repent!"

The approach of that dreaded red and white surcoat froze the guards in terror. Most of them died before they remembered how to defend. The others only survived because an eruption of five thousand Turks from the nearby woods distracted the French from their task.

The Turkish captain, a marvelously huge knight named Cornyfer, led the charge. "Fools," he cried. "You came to save this man from the Admiral's justice? 'Twas a great mistake, for now you shall hang at his side!"

Roland spun toward the Turk like an enraged lion, with Durandal bright in his hand.

Cornyfer was a very great champion and not a man to be intimidated. He lashed out with a sword as tall as a man, timing his blow to use the force of Roland's charge against him. The impact drove the knight's iron shield down with a resounding *Gong!* like the peal of a giant bell, and frightened his horse so badly that it began to buck and wheel. Roland yanked desperately on the reins, trying to regain control.

Cornyfer cut a second time, this time from behind. Roland felt it more than he saw it, and threw his shield blindly over his head. The stroke landed like a falling tree and sent a shivering numbness all the way down to the knight's fingers. The third blow he had to parry with Durandal. It would have slain his horse beneath him.

There was no fourth stroke, however. Cornyfer rode close with sword raised high, but Roland had mastered his mount. The Champion of France stood in his stirrups, brushed the heathen's guard aside, and struck a blow so ferocious that it split Cornyfer's head and chest in half, and still had enough force to slice through the saddle and slay the Turk's horse as well. The charging soldiers blanched with horror as their Captain fell in two pieces to either side of his dying mount. Roland took the opportunity to race back toward his friends by the gallows.

The Turks recovered quickly, as was their wont. They pressed forward, howling with vengeful rage, but the Frenchmen closed behind their leader and held the enemy off. Roland leapt down from the saddle, removed the hood and began to work at the knots that bound Guy. He'd just finished when a single Turk broke through the ring and spurred to attack the dismounted knights.

Guy saw the man coming and yelled, "Roland, beware!"

It was a sight Guy never forgot. As the Turk's sword descended from behind, Roland moved in a graceful swirl that drew his sword, deflected the blow, thrust up to the enemy's vitals, and then hurled him from the saddle like a sack of laundry, all in one fluid motion. Then he smiled at his younger cousin. "Aren't the ways of God wonderful to behold? Here I was, worrying about your being afoot, and not a moment later He provides you with a mount."

Guy laughed and stepped into the empty stirrup.

THE TURKS surrounded the knights tightly, struggling to break through the ring of defense, but the French maintained such good order and cooperated so marvelously well that the heathens could make no dint. Soon all were enmeshed and almost unable to move. It was Guy of Burgundy who won the day. He tore into the enemy crying out, "Now you will see I am *truly* free!"

Four men fell in as many seconds, and the Turks, abashed, drew back to a bowshot's range. The Admiral saw this from afar and began to sense another disaster in the offing. With a sharp command he sent reinforcements streaming out from Aygremore.

"Lords," cried Roland, "now is the time to retire. We must advance on the Tower bridge. With an effort we may yet save ourselves."

The company turned but Guy called out, "Did we not come out yesterday to gather food? Let us not leave the task half done! After today they will besiege us as though we were each a thousand men. Better to die fighting now than hear again, a few weeks hence, the lamentations of ladies who lack for bread."

The others could only agree, so as the Turks massed before the bridge to slow the knights' escape, they wheeled about and charged in the other direction – right at the reinforcements who'd thought they were attacking from behind.

The Saracens shattered and splintered into chaos, which allowed the French to rampage back and forth over the field. The ladies cheered them on from the high Tower windows, waving their filmy scarves. Floripas was so filled with joy at Guy's feats that she cried out in a loud voice, "Oh valiant knight, seeing your prowess I know it is my father in danger and not us!" Greatly cheered, the Peers rode again and again through the milling foe.

Suddenly Floripas called, "Look, my love! Over there!"

The knights followed her finger and saw an even larger train than the one they'd taken the day before – forty wains laden with bread, meat and wine. They whirled as one, and as one rode down the guards. Before the Admiral could even react, they were safe in the Tower with all the supplies in tow.

IT MAY WELL be imagined that the Admiral was less than happy when he saw Guy of Burgundy, who had been in his power, not only free but also back with his fellows; and more, that they were all now furnished with great abundance. He drove his servants off with a sword and demanded the presence of Brullant, Sortibrant and his other councilors.

"My Barons," he said as they arrived, "you have seen how harshly these Frenchmen have dealt with us thus far, and now they have garnished the Tower with enough bread, wine and other victuals to last for months. If word of this should somehow reach Charles we would be hard pressed. He would come to their aid with all his armies, and his might and puissance, as well you know, are so great as to threaten us all. Wherefore I am greatly concerned and in need of your wisdom."

To this Sortibrant answered, "I counsel that every man be armed with great show and mighty engines be erected as if we planned to assail the Tower by force. If we sound a thousand trumpets at once, with great drums as well, the French will be so dismayed that we could enter the Tower at our leisure and ease."

Brullant replied angrily. "My friend, you speak like a fool! You cannot believe that horns and drums could frighten the men in that Tower. The flower of France lies within those walls!

"Roland is in there, whose might and courage are so great that all who stand before him are sure to die. Beside him is Oliver, who conquered the champion of all Pagans in single combat. Is there a one of us that holds a candle to Fierabras' sun?

"And beside them? Ogier the Dane, Thierry of Ardennes, Guy of Burgundy and Gerard of Montdidier. Duke Naymon himself is there! You think to frighten such men as those with horns and drums? That is Roland, in there. *Roland!* We have slain two, so now they are only ten, but if they were all such as he they would ride from that Tower and drive us into the sea by themselves, Charles or no Charles!"

At these words the Admiral waxed mightily wroth. Flushing with rage, he wrenched his sword from its scabbard and would have struck Brullant dead but for the intervention of Sortibrant, who caught his hand. "Sir Admiral, leave off your anger. Let us rather turn our attention to how this Tower might best be assailed."

"I will tell you how," said the Admiral viciously. "Summon Mephistus the Enchanter."

Every king around the table blanched and whitened at that command, but no one spoke a word of protest.

THE NEXT morning, innumerable horns shattered the air as the Saracen army gathered around the Tower. Fighting men filled the land for a mile in every direction. But this was not the worst, for the Enchanter Mephistus had arrived to break down the walls by means of his art. Under his command huge engines had been built during the night, with iron shields to protect the men inside from any weapons the defenders might hurl. Now, to the sound of horns and drums, the engines crept slowly forward toward the knights' redoubt.

While still a hundred yards short of the moat, Mephistus' devices began to fling gigantic stones that broke the Tower's outer wards to piles of rubble, which quickly filled the moat. The furious knights could do nothing to impede this process.

At noon the bombardment ceased and the Saracens attacked once again. This time they poured forth in numbers against the gate itself, which they'd not been able to do before. Even lacking its outer defenses, however, the Tower was so strongly built that the enemy could find no means to enter. Moreover, the defenders cast down a hail of arrows, stones, spears and other objects that slew wherever they fell. After a day of this the attackers once again fell back in confusion and dismay.

A day later the Enchanter returned with new engines. These hurled balls of flame that, by his craft, set fire to the pillars and stones of the Tower itself. The helpless knights inside could only watch as the draw-bridge collapsed open with a boom, leaving just the iron portcullis to guard the passage into the Tower. "We are doomed," muttered Geoffrey of Anjou. "We have no means to defend ourselves against an assault such as this."

"Nay my lord, be of good heart," said Floripas. "Do not despair until you have seen the end of things come finally to pass. For I know the means by which these flames artificially burn the stone, and I know how to stop them as well."

With her ladies and the knights to run and fetch, Floripas collected certain herbs and medicines, then set them to steep in a keg of wine. The knights looked worriedly out the window but were soon forced back. The heat from the burning stone was such that the air was almost too hot to breathe. They voiced no impatience, however. As Duke Naymon reminded them, "Our fate now rests in the lady's art more than our hands. We must trust that she will act as soon as may be."

The flames had climbed up the walls and could be seen through the high window when Floripas finally directed the men to pour her beverage on the fire. Fighting the heat, they obeyed.

Silence erupted as loud as the fire's roar had been. The potion's first touch wholly extinguished the blaze.

The Admiral almost died of anger when he saw the flames disappear. When he heard it was the work of Floripas he swooned three times from sheer rage. "Mahon forbid I ever eat another bite until I see her torn asunder for this!"

King Brullant answered, "If that is what you'd accomplish Sire, then sound the horns to assail the Tower without delay. Remember the wisdom of King Corsuble, so sadly lost at Rome: 'Nothing defeats an army faster than its own delay.'

"We are all fresh, while those within have already fought a long day's battle against a foe they couldn't touch. Let us recommence the assault and give no way until the French are vanquished at last. You can be sure they have but few more darts and shot with which to resist."

"It shall be so," said the Admiral grimly. He gave the signal and a great fanfare rose from all the thousand trumpets about the Tower. The Saracens charged again.

This renewed attack was so great that the air grew dark with arrows, stones and other engines of destruction. The weakened outer walls tumbled to the earth as uncountable thousands of armed men charged toward the Tower gate. In truth, at this point the French had no more darts and arrows but what they could retrieve from those who assailed them. More than one voice began to rise in prayer, begging God to grant the speaker His grace of a worthy death. Then Floripas stepped forward.

"Lords, do not dismay! This Tower is yet strong enough to sustain us if we use the weapons at hand."

"What weapons are those, fair one?" said Ogier. "We've naught left but the swords in our hands."

"Only this," she answered. "Do you forget the high room wherein the gods watch over the treasure of my father? It contains great wedges and plates of gold and bullion. Let us go fetch those. We can as easily slay the enemy with metal as we can with stones – aye, and better!"

Guy of Burgundy, her love, swept her up, spun her about, and then kissed her soundly on the lips. The knights cheered loudly but neither of the pair seemed to hear.

The entire group then dashed to the room where the pagan gods lay scattered and broken. Each of the knights and maidens gathered a great quantity of treasure, then went to the battlements and began to hurl it down to the pain and dismay of the attacking soldiers. It took only a moment before the Saracens realized with what they were being assaulted. The men instantly forgot both their intent and discomfiture, and began to slay their fellows in greed for a share of this great abundance.

The Sultan became so mad with anger that he almost died where he stood. He foamed at the mouth and turned many colors, all the while screaming in a high voice, "Leave off the assault! Retreat! *Retreat!!*"

ADMIRAL BALAN spent the rest of the day weeping with anguish and rage. "My gods, you betray me! I left my treasure in your care, the which took me great pains to collect, yet now these French hurl it from the walls to my ruin! And how much more will I lose if we take up the battle again?" He kicked at an idol of the god Margotte. "I'll never trust your word again!"

"Do not blame the gods, Sire" said Sortibrant. "These French are cunning, like thieves. They must have stolen your treasure by trickery."

None can say if the Admiral accepted this explanation, but it did nothing to calm his fury. The horns continued to sound the retreat, and again he went to his bed with the Tower held by the Frenchmen within.

CHAPTER 10 – THE RIDE OF RICHARD OF NORMANDY

While the Admiral spent his time in rest and rage, the knights continued to work. Enemy soldiers could have slipped into the lower levels during the assault, and many continued to creep about outside in search of coin their fellows had missed. This threat required a room-by-room search. After that, they had to contrive a repair for the broken portcullis, new barriers to replace the drawbridge that could no longer be raised, and some manner of reinforcement for the many-holed Tower walls. Only when this work was done could they sit in conference over their captured supplies.

"Comrades," said Richard of Normandy as they wearily chewed their bread, "we have done all that we can to keep the enemy outside these walls, but those same defenses enclose us ever tighter within. Sooner or later we will fall to a siege so great. Wherefore it seems wise to me that we should send to the Emperor for aid. Without it our death is inevitable."

"You speak a folly," said Duke Naymon. "There is no man here that would take such a message. The land is filled with innumerable foes. He who left could not possibly survive to deliver our plea. Better to trust in Providence for delivery from the fate you foresee – which I cannot dispute – than to waste our strength and lives on a hopeless mission."

"All I can add," said Floripas, "is that you should fill what time we have left with as much joy as you can. You have here twenty fair maidens; let each of you take one at his pleasure."

The younger knights, including Roland, Oliver and several others, rejoiced at this suggestion and thanked Floripas with words of great praise, but Duke Thierry of Ardennes interrupted them angrily.

"Sirs, you have seen with what great numbers we shall be shut in. And there can be no doubt that we shall eventually be overrun. We must do as Duke Richard suggests and send a messenger to Charles."

"That is all well and good, but who would risk such a fate?" asked Ogier.

Roland stood. "I will."

"*NO!!*" This burst from many throats, but it was Duke Naymon who put their concerns to words. "Of us all, Sir Roland, you are the one who must *not* go. The Pagans' dread of your hand is half our defense. If they discovered you gone, the Admiral's host would drown us like the tide. We could stack bodies like hay in the harvest and still they would not pause."

Roland sat grudgingly. Several other knights immediately stood and volunteered to go in his place – including Guy of Burgundy, though his name was withdrawn when Floripas would not consent. After many disputations it was the arguments of Richard of Normandy that finally held sway.

"My lords, you know that I am blessed with a son of great noblesse who, as I suppose, is valiant in arms already. If I am slain in delivering this message, he will receive my heritage, hold it, and continue our service to Charles. How many of you can say the same?

"But more, hasn't the Emperor dealt more generously with me than he has with anyone else?" That prompted a storm of protests but he held up a hand and forged on.

"Did he not grant me a Duchy, even when I refused to accept it until he'd confirmed our ancient law: That any man, be he thrall or slave, who dwells a year in Norman land is thereafter free forever? Did he not heap me with honor and riches despite that defiance? Who but I, then, should undertake this perilous task?

"And finally, while I grant the presence in this company of arms as strong as mine, who among you would compete with me for saddle-skill alone?" No one answered, for Duke Richard had justly earned his fame as the finest rider in the Kingdom. "Speed will matter more than strength in so desperate an envoy as we now consider. I am the best choice to serve as messenger."

When the others had at last agreed, Duke Richard bowed his head. "Your tears do me honor but we have no time for sorrow. Let us plan how I should depart. If the Saracens discover my passage I could not possibly resist them."

"A diversion should be easy enough to manage," said Roland. "If we rise with the light and make a sortie the Sultan's guard will assault our passage with such vigor as to loose their watch on the Tower. I've little doubt you could then depart in secrecy while the rest of us lead them on a merry chase. When enough time has passed, and we have sufficiently done our desire, we shall return to safety and pray for your success."

So it was agreed, but so it was not to be. When the company gathered by the gates in the morning they beheld a force of countless Saracens crowded so thickly around the Tower bridge that a charge was impossible. They were truly and properly trapped.

TWO MONTHS passed in this way. The Admiral would not attack, but he massed his guards so tightly about the Tower that the Peers were pinned within. The break finally came when the Admiral lost patience and chose to go hunting with many of his kings. With their captains away the soldiers' diligence relaxed. Sharp-eyed Ogier, watching from a high window, noticed the difference and quietly summoned the French to don their armor.

The shock of the knights' charge shattered the boggling cordon. The pursuit began slowly but soon gathered up the whole of the surrounding force. First hundreds, then thousands of Saracens flew vainly after the racing group like a mob of starlings pursuing a hawk.

Duke Richard, half blinded with tears, waited in the Tower until the last guard had joined the chase. Then he softly left in their wake and spurred his horse for the hills that ringed the city. He rode without pause to the very peaks before pausing to rest.

A lesser rider would not have made half that distance but Richard was unique, as the other Peers had acknowledged. Even so, by the time they finished the climb his mount was shaking so hard that it could barely take the final steps.

Looking down, the Duke saw the French retire in good order to the Tower and breathed a prayer of thanks. The sight lightened his heart. Only briefly, however, for a long journey lay ahead. He slipped from the saddle to attend to his exhausted horse.

It was at this moment that fortune had her laugh.

THE SUN emerged suddenly from behind a cloud and framed Richard's image on the hilltop. The movement as he dismounted was just enough to catch the eye of the Saracen King Brullant and his hunting companions.

"Sortibrant, Clarion, look!" he said. "That can be no one but one of the French, a messenger to Charles seeking aid. Let us gather some troops to take him captive."

"By my oath, we shall not!" said King Clarion. "One of those Frenchmen slew my champion and friend, Rampyr. I shall not be content until my own sword rests at this one's throat."

Sortibrant remonstrated with the younger man as he pulled on his armor. "Don't be a fool! In a few minutes we could have a thousand troops at our side. Why not be safe and sure about this man's capture?"

"You may run for help if you wish, but I am riding to battle," answered Clarion. He climbed back into his saddle, yanked the reins wickedly about, and charged up the hill. Sortibrant watched with dismay as he left.

Brullant placed an understanding hand on his friend's shoulder. "Go. I will render what aid I may to our impulsive companion while you bring up support. The messenger will no doubt be captured by the time you return, but it would be good to have chains with which to bind him."

He spurred after Clarion with a loud blast on his hunting horn. In this effort he was quickly frustrated, however, for the younger King owned an enchanted saddle that gave his charger the strength to race without tiring for thirty leagues. So mounted, the Admiral's nephew easily outdistanced Brullant over the difficult terrain.

Richard of Normandy jumped at the sound of an approaching horn, and then gasped as if struck by a strong blow to the stomach. Two armored knights were riding toward him, the leader on a mount that raced over the ground like a bird on the wing. Meanwhile his own horse, the noble Doulstyn, still blew with exhaustion.

Flight was impossible, delay would be fatal, and he could already see a thousand more shapes stirring further downhill beneath the forest canopy. His soul chilled at the sight. But no Duke of Charlemagne was a man to be ruled by his fears. Richard stroked Doulstyn's proud neck with a murmured apology, and then mounted to face the foe.

CLARION rode his enchanted horse into the meadow with a thirty-foot leap that cleared both a massive boulder and a screen of small trees. "Hold, Messenger! Here shall your errand fail, as shall the thread of your life!"

"What trespass have I done to you that you should accost me so?" answered Richard. "Leave me be and I promise to remember your kindness."

Clarion raised his shield and pulled out his sword. "In a few minutes you'll be past remembering or forgetting anything." He spurred his mount to a savage attack.

Richard could feel Doulstyn trembling beneath him. He knew the stallion couldn't withstand the shock of a fresh charge. Nevertheless, he urged the good steed forward and rose in the stirrups as if to meet his opponent strength-to-strength and shield-to-shield.

Clarion smirked inside his helmet as the distance closed. The Christian had lost his nerve! His mount was shying from the impact of a clash. It was a bit of cowardice for which Clarion would make him pay dearly.

He closed on Duke Richard with his sword held high. Adding the speed of his charge to the force of his cut, he drove a blow that crashed through his opponent's weakened guard. The Frenchman reeled in his saddle.

A sharp command to his mount brought them spinning around as they passed, parallel to the messenger and slightly behind. Clarion's sword rang down a second time on the Richard's helm. This time the older man sagged.

Clarion grinned triumphantly. "Now you die!" he cried. He rose in the stirrups for the final blow.

Richard had expected nothing less. With Doulstyn in such a condition he couldn't hope to win a normal duel. Besides, he couldn't afford the time, not with a second man approaching and an army stirring below. So he'd traded those blows – deliberately weakened his defense – for the position he wanted. The two mounts now stood essentially still, side by side and facing the same direction. Clarion was a little behind him, on the shield side. The plan could still work if Richard could only clear his head in time.

Clarion roared an exultant war cry and drove down the killing blow, secure in the knowledge that it couldn't be blocked from that height and angle.

Richard knew it too, so he didn't try. Instead he dropped his shield hand to the horn of his saddle and threw his inside leg – the one between the horses – back and over the high cantle seat.

Clarion's sword sped past Richard's moving thigh and smote the spot he'd just abandoned. Sparks erupted from the iron shield. Richard, meanwhile, swung beneath Doulstyn's wide barrel, burst up between the two horses, and stabbed the lightly armored spot at the pit of his enemy's extended arm. The Saracen collapsed with an agonized cry, his own dead weight driving the blade even deeper. Richard paused a moment to catch his breath and then heaved the body down like a bale of hay on a one-handed pitchfork.

Brullant, now less than a hundred yards away, howled with dismay but knew he'd come too late for vengeance. The victorious Frenchman vaulted lightly into Clarion's empty saddle and raced off down the other side of the mountain. Brullant could do nothing but watch the fleeing back vanish into the trees. He reined up, uttered a curse, and sounded his horn for aid.

SARACENS began to arrive on the spot within a few minutes. They came by the hundreds, but they were as helpless as King Brullant. The majority simply covered their faces and set up a great cry of mourning. Others tried to catch the reins of Richard's horse, but soon discovered that Doulstyn would never abide the touch of a heathen hand. With his reins flying behind him, the good steed wound his way back down the mountain toward the Tower where he'd been stabled for the past many months.

When the Admiral saw the riderless horse he rejoiced to the Kings around him. "By my god Apollo, see you there? My nephew Clarion has slain the French messenger! From this moment he stands highest of you all and dearest to my heart.

"You men," he ordered. "Bring me that stallion."

This doubled the number of pursuing soldiers but added nothing to their success. Despite all their efforts, the noble Doulstyn escaped to the Tower. The knights who'd remained met him with the deepest grief.

Duke Naymon spoke first. "Richard of Normandy, sore shall you be missed! And no less because your fall means that we shall have neither aid from the King nor help from your party in France."

Roland, Oliver and the others, hearing these words, wept bitter tears. Only Floripas had comfort to offer.

"By God's honor, my lords, leave your lamenting and sorrow until we know the whole truth of this matter. For I judge by the sounds outside that more has happened than we might guess."

At her words the Peers noticed that the noise from beyond the gate had softened from a triumphant roar to a waiting silence. They hastened upstairs to a window and saw a large party coming down the mountain-side, bearing a burden toward the Admiral's flag. The entire Saracen army echoed the shriek of dismay that followed its arrival.

Within the walls a grinning Floripas turned to Roland. "Would you know why the Saracens show such sorrow? Richard has slain King Clarion and won his enchanted saddle. So mounted, he could outfly a bird on the wing! Nothing but Mantryble can stop him now."

Oliver leapt forward and grasped Roland in a joyous embrace. "You cannot know how glad I am of these tidings! My very soul rings sure; our danger has passed. We could be no safer now in the strongest castle of France! Blessed be Richard of God, for he's born himself nobly in-deed."

The other knights joined their praises to Oliver's and then, teary-eyed with joy, looked back out the window. The day suddenly seemed brighter than it had but a few minutes before.

WHEN THE Admiral heard of his nephew's death, he swooned three times and fell to the earth in a trance. He lay there for many minutes, bereft of his senses, as the Saracens indulged in a great weeping and lamentation. When he woke, though, orders were ready on his lips. He quickly called for a messenger.

"Go to Mantryble and give these letters to Galafer, the warden. Say to him that since it was he who suffered the knights of Charles to come over the Bridge, the which have caused us much grief and annoyance, it shall be he who bears the responsibility for their actions. Tell him further that one of the French goes thither on an errand to Charles, and that if he succeeds, my throne may be as threatened as my Tower. Charge him, therefore – on pain of death – to keep the Bridge so well that neither man, nor hart, nor hound, nor hare may pass over."

RICHARD arrived at Mantryble that evening and found the gates of the city barred for the night. Exhausted though he was from the day's journey and duel, he nevertheless pushed onward, searching far up and down the torrential River Flagot in search of a ford. He found nothing. Upstream the river ran deep and fast, while downstream it exploded in wide, impassible rapids. He returned to a vantage overlooking the city just in time to see the messenger arrive from Balan and to hear the city bells begin their alarm. A short time later, an army of fifteen thousand men poured from the gates and began to search the land.

"They know I'm here," he said quietly. "What shall I do now? If I fight, they will strike off my head. If I enter into this hideous river I shall be drowned and lost. Yet if I return to my fellows it would be a great default to Earl Roland, who holds my vow to deliver this message through all trials."

He pondered in this way for several minutes, searching for another solution, but found none. "Very well. It shall be success or nothing." He urged his horse down the hill and toward the foaming rapids.

This movement caught the eye of a Saracen troop led by the giant Mandysee, Galafer's brother. Mandysee was as black as pitch, seven feet in girth, and twice the height of a man, though still the smaller of the two. He called, "Hold messenger! You have ridden too far already. The shade of King Clarion cries out for vengeance. Now he shall have it!" He motioned for his archers to loose their bows at the fleeing knight.

One of the shafts caught in the high cantle of Richard's saddle and several more whirred past his ear, but none did lasting damage. With the aid of the saddle's enchantment Richard's mount easily outraced the cordon to the river's bank. At that point, however, he was trapped. The searchers spread out behind to cut off his escape. Their shrill horns rang through the air to summon ever more hunters to tighten the net.

Duke Richard urgently searched the bank, desperate for some hint of a way across. There was nothing. The river, still wider than a bow could shoot, flew by faster than a crossbow's bolt. Here and there it exploded against huge boulders with stunning plumes of white violence. No boat ever made and no swimmer ever born could have survived that current for a minute. Richard had only his horse and his wits.

He was almost ready to despair when another flight of arrows whirred by. This disturbed a white hart from a small copse of bushes nearby. It bounded away from the attack and down toward the stream.

At the bank it paused, looked up at the Norman Duke, and then stepped daintily into the torrent where it danced precariously from huge, wet stone to huge, wet stone.

"It's a miracle," Richard whispered. Then he sat up straight and his eyes widened. "It *is* a miracle!"

Commending his soul to heaven, the knight spurred his horse into the deadly flood.

His pursuers watched helplessly, abashed. No mortal steed could have traced the white hart's path. But this one had a magic saddle to sustain it. No mortal rider could have driven a mount into the churning foam, guided it from leap to leap, nor stayed in the saddle while it did. But this was Richard of Normandy. It should have been impossible but he did it nevertheless.

Almost.

Ten bounds from the further shore, the Saracen horse reached its limits. Even the enchanted saddle could sustain it no longer. Right between two steps it gave a sudden shiver, staggered and then collapsed. Richard leapt free and disappeared into the flood.

Search parties dispatched by Galafer found the mount hours later, a mile downstream and battered almost to pieces by the water's force. Of the messenger they found no sign. The Saracen giant retired to his chambers and prayed to his gods, but found there little comfort.

THE CAMP and court of Charlemagne, King of the Franks and Emperor of the West, had divided into factions as the months dragged on and the King spent ever more time in seclusion. The depth of this division became clear when he at last called his barons in to council.

"My lords and friends," he began, "I am much troubled. The cause is apparent. It was I who sent so many of my special barons as messengers to the Admiral Balan. It is I who am responsible for their loss. We have idled here these many months waiting for news, but neither word nor tidings has come.

"The fault is mine. I am no longer fit to lead you. Take this crown. Take it! I depose myself from the throne."

These words filled Ganelon with relief, for his family had become ever more strident in their desire to abandon the campaign. *The missing men are no loss to us. Let us return and claim what we can from their absence.* As the family spokesman he had resisted this infamous suggestion. Indeed, he had paid a heavy price for doing so, one that the King would never know. This solution answered all problems. His family could gain its desire without any compromise to Ganelon's personal honor.

None of these feelings appeared on his face as he said, "Sire, my advice would be to delay this decision and instead give orders to take up our tents and return to France. The land of Aygremore is passing strong; the Admiral is of great fierceness; and both he and the other pagans bear you a special grievance by reason of his son Fierabras' conversion to the True Faith. Let us return then to France, where there are children who shall, in the course of time, wax great enough in arms to replace those barons you have lost."

This he said with a telling glance at his cousin Aloys, who not-so-secretly coveted the lands those children stood to inherit. "It may take twenty years, but they shall be with us when we return to Spain to recover the bones of Roland, the noble earl for whom you mourn above all others."

These words smote the King with so great a sorrow that he swooned and could not speak for the space of an hour. Bitterly he said to himself, *'You poor, miserable wretch, what shall you do? Return and be dishonored? You would be better dead than shamed in such a way. They cannot love you who counsel such a course.'*

When at last he came to himself his barons were still there. "You have heard the words of Ganelon, which give me no pleasure. If I return now, without avenging my Peers, what man could trust me thereafter? They would see only shame, and rightfully so."

Ganelon's friends and family, including Zachary, Aloys, Aubrey and several others, reacted to this with anger. "Sir Emperor, do not think to take any course but that which Ganelon has so wisely counseled. We brought twenty thousand men at your command, but with Roland and the others dead they have lost their heart for the fight. If you purpose to go anywhere but back to France you will do it without them and without us."

Duke Reyner, Oliver's father, rose in protest. "My King, if you believe these words your guidance shall be so evil that all of France shall be brought to ruination. Is it possible that men such as Roland, Ogier, Oliver and Naymon could be slain without some sign or portent? No! By this we may know that they live. You must therefore ride forward, to songs of glory, not back to the tune of craven counsel. Those who say otherwise see only a path to their own gain. They pass lightly over the harm they would cause."

Aloys surged forward, spitting with fury. "Reyner of Atri, your words are lies! If the King were not present you would pay for them with your head. We know well what you are: your father Garin was but a poor man of low condition and you are no better than he. Your words count no more than a slave's."

Duke Reyner was never a man to suffer such an injury without taking action. He dove at Aloys and smote him to the ground with a fist.

After that, confusion reigned supreme. The two men rolled on the earth, while others roared and fought above them. Someone would surely have died had Charlemagne not been present to prevent the drawing of steel. Even then, it required the mass and might of Fierabras to separate the combatants long enough for the King to make himself heard.

"Hold where you are! By my crown, the next person to strike a blow shall be hanged as a thief whatsoever may be his estate!"

"Reyner," swore Aloys viciously as he wiped at his nose, "it may not happen here or now, but your life shall be mine when we return to France."

"Say not so," interrupted the King. "You shame me, Aloys, to make such threats in my Court. Retract them now and make your amends or you'll answer to me where we stand."

Aloys glared bitterly at Duke Reyner for a long moment, then slowly dropped to his knee and begged the Duke's pardon. No sooner had he done so than another great commotion began, this time outside the pavilion. One of the guards cried out, "Hold! You can't go in there! What do you think... !"

The guard never finished his challenge. Instead he came hurtling back through the door, crashed into Aloys, and sent both of them sprawling to the ground. A strange apparition followed the guard in – a filthy, gray-haired savage who pushed by all that sought to restrain him and then bent his knee to the King.

Furious, Aloys snatched the guard's fallen sword and would have slain the beggar where he knelt but for Ganelon's holding him back.

Then the figure spoke in a voice as dusty as his clothes. "Sire, I have returned."

"Richard!"

CHAPTER 11 – THE BATTLE OF MANTRYBLE BRIDGE

The sudden arrival of one of the missing knights – grimy, bedraggled and exhausted as he was – set every heart to racing. "Good baron," asked the King eagerly, "how is it with you? What has become of my nephew Roland and my other Peers? Have you come alone? Are they alive or dead? Tell me, I pray you."

Excitement spread through the tent and camp as Duke Richard's tale spun out. "Sir Emperor, Roland and the others were whole and healthy when I left, though besieged in the strong Tower of Aygre-more by the Admiral of Spain. More than a hundred thousand Saracens ring them tightly. It was a miracle that I escaped with our plea for aid. The Admiral, who I assure you is a fierce and terrible man, has sworn by his gods Mahon and Termagant to never depart from the siege until those trapped in the Tower are hanged by the neck.

"With your knights are Floripas, the courteous daughter of the Admiral and the fairest maid in all the world, and twenty of her ladies. These have all sent you word by me begging for your aid – and if it pleases you to grant that aid, offering their powers that you may more quickly conquer both the country of Spain and all the lands beyond."

"Good Duke, your words bring me a greater joy than you can imagine. Enough discussion! Let all men of courage now ride, for Roland and the others await!"

Whatever may have hid in his heart, Ganelon raised as lusty a cry as the rest and joined the streaming barons as they raced to gather their men. Only Richard of Normandy tarried behind to catch the King for a final word.

"If you please Sire, I must speak with you of Mantryble. It is a dread fortress and unlikely to fall by storm. Nevertheless, I have a thought…"

GALAFER, the giant warden of the Mantryble Bridge, scowled down at the band of five hundred wealthy merchants, and especially their gray-bearded leader. "Vassal!" he boomed, "what is your name and what is the purpose that brings you here?"

"Sir," said Duke Richard, for it was he in disguise that stood before the giant, "I and my comrades are merchants from Tarragon who bear a great quantity of cloth and draperies. By the aid of Mahon, we hope to sell these goods at the faires by Aygremore. We also bring precious gifts for the Sultan. What counsel can you grant us to further this venture?"

Galafer was suspicious enough but felt no fear. The man before him was clearly old and past the days of adventure. He was also less than half of Galafer's size, unarmored, and the bridge that the giant defended was as invincibly strong as any the mind of man had ever conceived. The roadway of the Mantryble Bridge was wide enough for twenty knights to ride abreast but the points of entry at either end, both here at the river's edge and across the way at Mantryble City, were contained by marvelously strong towers and huge drawbridges equipped with heavy iron chains. Golden eagles flamed proudly in the morning sun at the top of each Tower. In between were thirty strong, marble arches to support the bridge, all of which had iron bars that defenders could drop at need.

"You may not pass," Galafer bellowed. "The Admiral has forbidden it. Not long since there passed hereby seven ruffians and rogues of France who were messengers of the Emperor Charles. They promised me a great tribute for their passage and have yet to pay. My lord the Admiral now keeps them in prison – all except one who escaped the other day, skulking like a thief, on the best horse I ever saw. He died in the River after slaying my cousin, King Clarion, for whom we greatly mourn. Would that Mahon, my god, had brought him here to this bridge...! I would have cleaved the dastard to his belly without mercy or pity.

"Since that escape the Admiral has great fear of treason. The more so because his son Fierabras has renounced Mahon to become Christian. He has therefore commanded me three times to deny passage to any person, be he lord, knight or servant. And further that I should search well all who come to be sure of their condition. Therefore I would know more of who and what ye be."

Richard bowed his head and struggled to think of some way to continue his deception.

Meanwhile, three of the Duke's most loyal retainers, Francoise, Felix, and their ward Philippe, walked softly over the way and crept toward the Tower gate. When Galafer saw them he was outraged. "What is this? I said that none shall pass!"

He immediately stepped to a gigantic wheel and drew up the drawbridge, cutting off the rest of their party. He had no dread of just four men.

"You are over bold to enter without my command. You shall be set in prison for this, along with any of your party that follows, and tomorrow I shall send you as prisoners to the Admiral for judgment. Now take off your cloaks, for you seem to me an evil sort and I would see what you hide beneath."

He grasped Francoise by the cloak and pulled sharply, spinning the unfortunate knight around four times.

"By God," said the hot-blooded Philippe with all the outrage of his beardless years, "You can't treat my cousin like that!" He threw off his cloak, drew his sword, and smote with all his strength at Galafer's side. The cut had no effect for the giant was armored with the hide of an old Serpent. Philippe followed quickly with a second blow, and then a third. They too skittered off.

Encumbered by Francoise's dangling form, Galafer reacted slowly at first. But once he'd caught his balance, he grabbed with his free hand for the boy who yapped and snapped about his knees like an annoying puppy. Philippe threw a desperate stroke at the tree-sized arm. The armor rejected the blow again, but this time the blade glanced up. Purely by chance, the tip reached in and snicked off a bit of the giant's ear.

Galafer roared with fury and threw Francoise into the younger man. Both went sprawling to the roadway. Duke Richard and the other Norman charged in from the other side before the giant could use his advantage. Galafer roared again and swept them aside with two swift cuffs. Then he stepped to the tower door and retrieved his man-sized, steel-headed axe. Twirling it lightly, he laughed at his four puny foes.

"Now you die!" he thundered.

The knights attacked as one. Galafer smote down at Philippe, who was still in the lead. The boy dodged to the side just in time. Wind from the huge blade pulled at his hair and clothes like a storm.

The other Normans launched a flurry of stabs and cuts but none had any more success with the Serpent-hide armor than young Philippe had enjoyed. Galafer ignored them, and wrenched the axe free in a shower of flying rock that sent the Frenchmen diving for cover.

'This is madness,' muttered Duke Richard from behind a pile of firewood. *'How can we fight or even grieve this monster if we can not cut through his armor?'* The Duke sheathed his sword as another blow of the axe sent knights tumbling about. In its place he grasped the heaviest log from the pile. Crying "God and the King!" he ran forward and drove it down on the giant's armored cap.

This new attack rocked the brute so much that he bellowed for aid. The city gate opened and belched ten thousand Saracens upon the Bridge. All of them raced to support their lord.

DUKE RICHARD ran to the huge wheel that raised and lowered the drawbridge. It was built for creatures of Galafer's size, and terribly hard to move. He strained desperately at the task while his three retainers hung on the giant's limbs like little Norman terriers besieging a bear. *'Never mind the enemy,'* Richard told himself fiercely, *'just move the wheel. Don't look. Just lower the bridge.'*

The wheel turned slowly, maddeningly, as the sound of heathen war cries came closer and closer. Richard labored until his arms were as hard as the marble walls and his heart pounded in his ears. The wheel refused to move any faster. The Saracen footsteps drummed on the road, growing louder with every beat. He knew that they'd arrive at any moment to overwhelm him and destroy all hopes. He strained even harder, until his world disappeared in a reddish fog of effort.

The sound of feet grew louder yet – and then vanished in the deafening thunder of hooves. All five hundred of the knights in Richard's command charged over the drawbridge and into the enemy force.

The heathens staggered back at the shock, firmed, and then continued to slowly retreat as the French pushed forward. Broad though it was, the Bridge was too narrow for armored knights to bypass the Saracen hoard. Richard's cavalry had no choice but to embark on the long, slow work of smashing through disciplined troops.

The battle edged away from the Tower gate and toward the first marble arch. Each side landed many grievous and mortal strokes. Duke Richard stood at the forefront, driving the enemy back with slashing cuts and powerful thrusts. He had no armor, however, for his disguise as a wealthy merchant had forbidden the wearing of mail. Bit by bit the nicks and cuts began to mount.

Behind him Galafer had shrugged off his opponents and was wreaking havoc with his monstrous axe. Knights and mounts fell to the great strokes with disturbing regularity. Ahead lay the stubborn mass of heathen troops.

Richard was weighing whether the giant or the army posed a greater threat, when a fresh roar came from the city. The gates opened and a second army poured to the Bridge, this one mounted and armed to match the French.

'I must get word to the King!'

The Duke fell back behind his men, dodged the chaos that surrounded the giant, and ran to a door inside the tower. He wrenched it open and flew up the stairs. When he reached the roof, he sounded three sharp blasts on his horn: the signal to summon King Charles. The French army raced from the concealing woods like greyhounds released from the slips.

From his high vantage Richard could see both sets of reinforcements converging on the vicious melee beneath. Everything now depended on speed, and he judged that the heathen had a narrow edge. The new force of Saracens would push his men into the foaming river if the French could move no faster. And if that happened they would raise the bridge and reduce the King's hopes to dust. Richard blew another triple blast, this one so urgent that the horn shattered on his lips.

From the center came Ganelon of Mayence. He hurtled ahead of the army with his flag unfurled and plunged into the press. A traitor he may have been in later days, but on this one he proved his worth. His reckless courage smashed the Saracen front and sent men fleeing back into the arriving city troops.

Richard cheered wildly and then leapt for the stairs to rejoin the fight. Ganelon's effort had bought the French twenty yards of road. That would be just enough.

THE SARACEN and French reinforcements collided with a thunderous crash that shook the earth. Duke Richard grasped a sconce for dear life to keep from being flung off the stairs. Many in the fray were less lucky. Soldiers from both sides fell by the dozens into the hungry, churning waters.

Charlemagne fought at the center. The press was particularly hot and furious in these confined environs. His famous blade Joyeuse smote rudely about, slaying whomever he faced. Ganelon and Richard fought at his side. They likewise did well their desire.

The slaughter continued for hours without pause. Bit by bit, however, the valiance of the French began to tell. Step by step, they advanced.

The shadows had begun to lengthen toward evening, carving the scene in sharp relief, when Charlemagne first caught sight of the city gate. Galafer, who was organizing the resistance, saw the waving Oriflamme approach. He brandished his massive axe in defiance.

"By Mahon, you dotard, you'd have been wiser to hide in Paris than to search for your doom by coming here! I shall take you to the Admiral, who will have no mercy. He will flay you alive, piece by piece – and I will be there to watch!"

Charles answered in a fury. "You will see nothing, villain, for I shall have your head before this day is done!"

The King set spurs to his stallion, urging him to one more charge through the enemy lines. Saracens clutched and grabbed at him like ticks for a dog but Joyeuse was a thing alive. The shining blade struck off the offending hands like so many stalks of grain. Ganelon, Duke Richard, and those of their folk who'd managed to stay together struggled to follow in his wake.

Galafer met the King with a monstrous blow of his axe. Charlemagne leapt from the saddle to avoid it, striking at the giant's arm even as he did. Joyeuse glanced harmlessly from the serpent's scales that protected the heathen's body. Not so the giant axe. The great steel head cut Charlemagne's abandoned horse completely in half and came out dripping from the other side.

"My lord," cried Richard as Charlemagne struggled away from another stroke of the man-sized axe, "strike for a gap! The armor can not be pierced."

The fury of the battle drowned his words completely. The King rushed in with a flurry of cuts, driving the backward even though none of the blows could reach his flesh. Such was the weight of Charlemagne's hand. But it was clear to the watching Richard that the King had caused no lasting harm. Nor would he. So long as Galafer remained on his feet, there was no unarmored spot for the King to reach even if he knew enough to look. The heathen was simply too tall.

They needed another plan.

Galafer recovered his balance and spun around before the Duke could find any ideas. He was amazingly fast for so huge a creature. The flat and haft of the axe shot out with stunning speed. Charlemagne caught a glancing blow that threw him down at the giant's feet. The heathen chortled and raised his weapon for the final stroke, but inspiration fell faster than his hand.

The same maneuver that surprised the King had turned Galafer's back to the Duke. Richard dove from the stirrups, drove his shoulder into the back of the giant's knees, and grabbed the enormous ankles. Galafer tottered, the killing stroke forgotten. Then Richard tightened his grip and stood.

"What...?!" The giant stumbled to his hands and knees.

Charlemagne allowed him no chance for further words. Joyeuse cut down at the exposed neck and clove it like a melon.

"God and the King!" called Richard triumphantly.

"God and the King!" cheered the French. They surged forward and the defenders broke at last, their courage fleeing with their champion's life. Saracens by the thousands began to run for the safety of the high city gates and walls.

Duke Richard helped the King to his feet, Joyeuse still dripping with Galafer's blood. "That was nobly done, your Majesty. Nobly indeed!"

"My thanks, good Duke. In the end it took two. But we have no time for this. We must take hold of the gatehouse, and soon, ere their panic ebbs. All it would take is one Saracen with a steady head and they'll have the drawbridge up and the portcullis down. The Bridge is nothing if we don't win the City as well. We must press on!"

Charles, Duke Reyner, Duke Richard, and Richard's Norman retainers cleared the building and then took up positions by the door to defend the way in. It was not long before the Saracens realized that their final wards had been compromised behind them. They mounted charge after charge in attempt to slay the little band and carry out exactly the plan that the King had foreseen.

The weight of numbers forced the French steadily back. In the last moment before they retreated into the gatehouse itself, Charlemagne rose up to his full height and yelled furiously over the attacking foes. "Frenchmen! Succor and aid! You must hurry!"

Then the Saracens pushed forward again and drove him inside with the others, away and out of view.

Ganelon heard the King's cry and immediately realized the stakes. *'If we don't relieve him at once they'll be cut off!'* He raised his horn to summon more men but a hand sped out and knocked it aside. He spun in his saddle and saw Aloys, his cousin.

"Don't be a fool," said Aloys. "We have fought and bled enough this day. Let others suffer the torments to come. What is it to us if Charles is trapped within? God forbid he ever departs! We shall thus have vengeance on him and Reyner both for the opposition they have given us. And when they are gone, yea, upon their subjects as well."

"God forbid I should ever do such treason to my rightful Lord!" said Ganelon. "We hold from him our lands and titles. False and faithless would I be named if I did as you suggest."

Aloys glanced at the hoard of seething Saracens and again leaned close. "You are a fool! Who could strip us of lands or titles when the King and his Barons are dead? With Reyner and Richard joining the King, the crown would be ours for the taking – yours, most likely. Let us depart, I say!"

Ganelon angrily shrugged off the restraining hand. "Never would I do such treason. Leaving the King in such peril would be the same as raising my hand against him. I'd rather be torn asunder than be guilty of such a deed."

Aloys was ill content at these words, and would have made a heated reply had Fierabras not come upon them in good array and great point. "Where is the King?" he demanded.

Ganelon spared a bitter look at his cousin and said, "Sir, we shall never see him again. He is enclosed within the gatehouse and dead by now, I suppose."

"You 'suppose?' You do not know and yet you tarry here? A man could name you traitor for this Ganelon, and fairly!"

Ganelon wordlessly raised his horn again and blew a loud summons. As he did, Fierabras stood in his stirrups so that he towered above all heads, and pointed his sword toward the gatehouse. "Behold!"

he roared. "The drawbridge is yet unraised and the King holds it with his life. To his aid, you French! On for the glory of Charles!"

"For Charles!" they answered. "On for the King!"

With Fierabras at the front and Ganelon at his side the French army swept past all resistance. The Saracens fought like famished wolves, but fell nevertheless. Such rivers of blood poured down the streets that men marveled to see it.

Aloys waited with his men outside the gate until he could see the battle was won. Then he hurried them in to the gatehouse and up the stairs. They took the last, desperate Saracens from the rear and hewed them down like so many sheaves of wheat.

"Sire," said Aloys, kneeling before the bloody and exhausted King, "through blood and pain, always will I ride to your aid."

Charles clapped a hand on Aloys shoulder and said, "Well done." He looked around the room at the Dukes Reyner and Richard, the Normans staggering from their wounds, and the kneeling men on the stairs behind the Mayencer noble. "All of you, well done."

IT WAS SOON discovered that Mantryble held great riches, for Admiral Balan had deemed it so strong and secure that he'd stored there a great part of his wealth. The army rested in the city for three days, as the King busily granted praise and rewards to all his subjects according to their station, quality and deeds. As always, his hand in these matters was so fair and liberal that all his men, both great and small, were well content.

Men with lesser duties spent the time sporting in the River Flagot and enjoying the gentle days,. Soon enough, however, Charlemagne called his peers in to council.

"My lords and barons," he said, "my heart is light with the smells of victory, but clouded nevertheless with fear for our special barons that lie yet imprisoned. Pleasant as this city may be, we must not tarry."

Duke Reyner stood and said, "Sire, my counsel is this. Your Baron Sir Raoul of Nantes was wounded in the side during the battle. Let him remain here with the other wounded and five thousand healthy men to hold the town and bridge. The rest of us can ride in the morning."

"Sire," added Raoul, "this is a task I would willingly accept. In truth, my wounds would make it difficult to ride to Aygremore."

Hearing no dissent, the King agreed.

Thus it came to pass that the next morning Charlemagne stood on a little hill outside the city with certain of his barons at his side. He watched proudly as the troops marched in good array from the site of one desperate battle to another that promised to be even worse. One of the men saw him and raised a cheer that spread up and down the miles-long line.

Tears filled the King's eyes. He looked up toward heaven and quietly said, "Nothing I have done could be enough to earn this grace. To command so mighty a people as this... ! With all my heart I give thanks and praise for the honor."

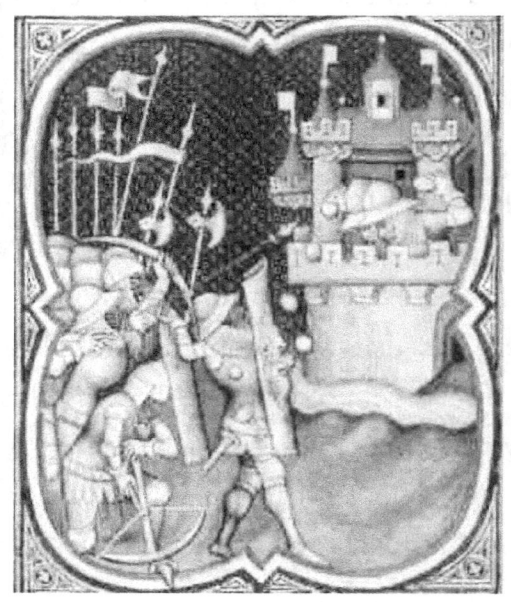

CHAPTER 12 – THE FINAL ASSAULT

Tidings of the terrible battle at Mantryble Bridge came quickly to Admiral Balan at Aygremore; of Galafer slain, the city lost, his treasuries sacked, and Richard of Normandy, who had been his captive, riding in the vanguard of the victorious French. He flushed at the news; first red, then purple, and finally black.

"Nnnoooooo!!"

Leaping to his feet, he raised his throne over his head, broke it to bits on the marble floor, and clutched the largest piece like a makeshift club. With this he brained the unfortunate messenger. Then he ran to the wall that sheltered his heathen idols. Weeping and screaming curses, he smashed the figure of Mahon in the face.

"Traitor god, your power is nothing! Only a fool would trust you after seeing my men slain and my treasures taken. You are nothing. Nothing!" The club crashed down again and again until the image toppled to the ground.

King Sortibrant hurried forward. "Sire, you must repent of this deed and make your amends to the god. He has a long memory for slights."

"Never! How could I bow my head to Mahon when he failed to protect my city and gold?"

"Whatsoever your opinion of the gods," said the more practical King Brullant, who had slipped up to join the two, "let us send out spies to inform us when the host of Charles comes hither against you. With all of your vassals here at Aygremore, I still believe we can take him captive and hang him by the neck with his people. The gods guard those who guard themselves," he finished.

"So it is said," admitted Sortibrant, "but if your Highness will apologize too, and bring the gods behind our effort, perhaps we can also capture Fierabras, your son. Then you may smite off his head and deal at your leisure with your daughter and the scoundrels who hold your Tower."

This image greatly cheered the Admiral. He returned to Mahon, righted the statue and humbly abased himself as Sortibrant desired. "As amends I shall increase thy worship in all lands and have made for thee a new form from a thousandweight of fine gold. And too," he added, "before the Emperor Charles can arrive you shall have my false daughter and her friends from the Tower as well."

"Summon the engines," he said to his kings. "We attack as soon as possible."

❧

THE ASSAULT began an hour later, more fervent than ever. The Saracen engines hurled gigantic stones against the Tower walls. Before long they'd made five new holes broad enough for a cart to pass through with ease. When the engines withdrew, the army moved in to exploit the ruined defense.

Oliver and Roland watched from a high window with their shields in front to ward off darts. Nervous fingers opened and closed on their sword hilts. Even those mighty hearts felt pangs of fear at the sight of so great an oncoming hoard. They and the others hurled down every stone and other missile they could find, but their efforts did no more damage to that ocean of men than the same might have done to the sea.

"My lords and brethren," said Roland, "now is the time to show our mettle. With heart, courage and discipline we may yet survive the day."

"Nay," said Oliver, "more than survive! Look, my brother. They have all come afoot, seeing that the holes in our walls need ladders to reach. We ten have been confined too long. Let us sally forth beneath them, as knights on horse, and see how they deal with that! I would rather die outside and be hewn from the saddle than be penned in here and cornered like some honorless beast."

Ogier the Dane instantly agreed with this plan. The others did too. Even Floripas encouraged their adventure. "Go my lords, and do your desire well. Our doors and wards will hold long enough against any who stray inside for you to finish the work without."

Greatly cheered by her words, the knights ran down the one remaining staircase they had not destroyed for the sake of defense. In moments their eager mounts were saddled and ready.

The leading edge of the Saracen army crested at the Tower's foot and began to force its way up the walls by sheer strength. Men climbed by hand where they could. Where hands wouldn't do they swarmed up dozens of ladders that rose like stalks of grass in a breeze. Floripas went to the high window and shook her fist defiantly at her father. "I might have known you'd need help to fight a woman!"

"Whore!" he screamed. "Putayne! He that brings me her head shall have my entire love and honor!"

The Saracen troops roared with eagerness and pushed up the ladders even faster. Then the Tower doors opened and death rode out from beneath.

The shock could not have been more profound. In one instant the Saracens were whooping with joy and lust. In the next they were toppling to their deaths, or standing on foot against mounted knights led by a fiend who wore red and white. They turned their tails and fled in terror, the Tower completely forgotten.

The French rampaged freely, lopping off heads like a boy lops flowers in a field, until the sun was low in the sky.

FURY AT the knights' defiance ate at the Admiral's heart, but with Charlemagne's army on the march he swore to press the assault regardless of cost. The French knights could guess this intent easily enough from the frothing screams that echoed through the dark. They accordingly worked at a feverish pace to patch where the walls had been holed the day before.

It did them little good. By noon the Saracen engines had reduced most of the Tower's front side to shattered ruins.

Under King Brullant's command, this day's attack had moderately less enthusiasm but considerably more in the way of order and purpose. Slowly, carefully, and in tight formations, the Saracens pressed on over the rubble. The steady chant of their pagan hymns sent shivers through the French who could do nothing but watch with a mixture of fear and frustration.

"Ma-HON, Ma-HON." "Ter-ma-GANT, Ter-ma-GANT."

Floripas interrupted the gloom with a sudden cry of delight. She leapt to her feet and excitedly said, "My lords, we forget the chamber that holds my father's gods! The coin may be gone, but there are other things to throw."

Ogier's grin matched her own. "I know just where to start."

The knights ran in to the Tower's depths while Floripas strolled to the window. Once again she leaned out and caroled taunts on her father's head. He erupted as if her voice was a white-hot prod.

"You are no daughter of mine, whore! When I finally take these wretched French, you shall burn at their side!"

Brullant ignored them both and kept the advance moving forward. But he began to feel uneasy.

Floripas called back, "Better to burn with noble oaks than to bathe in the muck and weeds. You were never my father. No mother of mine would have stooped so low!"

"Archers!" screamed the Admiral. "A bag of gold for the man who kills the whore!"

Brullant ground his teeth as men abandoned his careful formations for clearer shots. A quivering hail of bolts and arrows soared upward as Floripas ducked inside. She'd done what she could to buy some time. It wouldn't work again.

It took Brullant several precious minutes to regain control, even after the lady disappeared. Leaving a token force of fifty archers with her obsessed father, he whipped the other soldiers back into formation and started them marching again.

"Ma-HON, Ma-HON." "Ter-ma-GANT, Ter-ma-GANT."

By this time the knights were staggering back from the Admiral's treasure room. Floripas' eyes widened when she saw how Ogier had "improved" her idea. "I always say," he grunted, "that Heaven hears even a heathen's prayers."

He came to the window and called in a loud voice, "You want your gods? *Here!*"

With a mighty effort he and William the Scott heaved the treasury's massive statue of Termagant over the sill. Roland and Duke Naymon followed with the idol of Mahon, Oliver with the pieces of Margotte, and the others with as many bricks of gold and silver as they'd been able to carry.

The figures hurtled down and exploded on the boulders-strewn remains of the strong Tower walls. Fragments of gold and gems flew like bullets. Dozens of men fell dead or screaming in pain. The others stared in horror at the head of Mahon, severed from its body with one eye socket empty and the other staring lifeless and crazed.

When other gods began falling from the sky, the formations shivered like aspens in the breeze. One by one, the knights hauled them up and hurled them over the sill.

The end came when a brick of gold smashed Mahon's head like a grape beneath some mighty fist. Shrieking with superstitious terror, the heathen army scattered and ran once again.

THIS TIME the Admiral waxed so wroth that he swooned from sheer vexation. Brullant and Sortibrant had to carry him back to his tent on a litter, where he lay as if dead for more than an hour.

At last he stirred with a moan. "I am forsaken, failed by my gods at my greatest need! Mahon, you are old and a dotard, no fit god for any man."

"Sire," said Sortibrant, "it is an evil habit to speak ill of the gods. Mahon was angry with you for striking him on the nose with your club. Now, seeing what these Frenchmen have done, he will surely turn his anger on them."

"And there is this," added Brullant. "Gods or no gods, the Tower is empty of all they might throw. The enemy has nothing left but his swords. Howsoever puissant they may be, we have ten thousand blades for every one of theirs. Let us go forward again and press them. Press them, I say, by day and by night! Let the defenders neither sleep nor refresh themselves until they are taken and bound before you. If we trust in ourselves, the gods will surely follow."

Sortibrant spared him a look of reproach. "It is in Mahon we must trust and no other. Still, your advice is as good as ever. Sire, let us follow my brother's plan. Charles will be upon us soon. The heads of his knights would make an apt greeting."

"Let it be so," said the Admiral.

THE ASSAULT began that evening by torchlight. The first Saracens to reach the Tower met Roland and Oliver in the breach. They died. So did the wave that followed. But bit by bit the mass came on nevertheless.

The knights fought for every inch of hall and stair. With careful fore-thought they'd blocked off the rooms and ways that could have been used to bypass their defense, and erected various pillars and bars to prevent the enemy from using a table or other large shield as cover for the advance. Other barriers guarded against missiles from below. But nothing could change the weight of numbers. And nothing could grant the defenders a rest.

By sunrise the Saracens had pushed almost halfway up the Tower. Then word came from the ladies above: "Twenty thousand Turks come from the city to replace the men who fought in the night."

The Peers slumped tiredly behind a heavy door, wincing as much at the news at they did at the steady *Thump!* of the heathens' ram.

Duke Naymon, his white beard stained with blood and quivering with exhaustion, spoke quietly. "Old men are ready for death. It is you youngsters for whom I mourn."

"Mourn not for me, your Grace," said Ogier the Dane. "If I am to die it will be as a knight, with faithful heart and honor unstained. No treason or cowardice shall you have from me, my brothers. When I go my sword Cortana shall be in my hand and the heap of pagan dead shall be so high that men will marvel forever!"

Cries of *'Huzzah!'* rang through the chamber. Roland brandished Durandal, Oliver Hautclere, and each of the others his sword as well. Then the door flew suddenly inward as the ram drove it free from its hinges.

"Charles and honor!" cried Roland. He leapt forward with a joyous laugh, batted aside a spear, ducked beneath an axe, and was suddenly *there*; a whirl of death in the enemy's midst. Durandal glittered wetly as Roland danced – as *they* danced – knight and sword, together and one. The first man had barely fallen when the last choked out his life.

Roland shook the blade free of gore and slowly caught the eye of a Saracen at the end of the hall. He grinned.

The soldier shrieked, dropped his spear and bolted around a corner into the advancing troop of Turks. Roland pursued with the other Peers at his heels.

Naymon, at the rear, caught Duke Thierry by the arm. "Nineteen men," he counted. "Nineteen men, armed and ready, and they never had a chance. Sometimes it seems that God himself could envy that man's arm. Come! Let us see if he's left any for us!"

Laughing and greatly cheered, the paladins barreled down the hall.

EVEN HEROISM has its limits. In that charge the paladins regained a floor of the Tower and cleared a stair they'd lost, but the day wore on without relief. By noon the Saracens had hurled them back through the room where they'd started and another wave of fresh, rested troops had struck down William the Scot with a grievous wound that made him unable to fight. The rest of the day passed likewise. Not a man of the French but did his desire greatly. Every one proved his worth again and again in the long retreat. But a retreat it was nevertheless.

The sun was low and the knights were preparing their withdrawal to the final stair when a wordless shout came from the room above.

"That's Floripas!"

Duke Naymon bounded up the stairs and then called back to the others, "St. Denis! The flag of St. Denis has topped the hill!"

Charlemagne had arrived.

CHAPTER 13 – THE BATTLE OF AYGREMORE

The knights in the Tower rejoiced with tears and words of thanksgiving. An evening ago the enemy had pressed them to the limits of exhaustion and reached the very portal of their final redoubt. Then Charlemagne had arrived with his army, made camp in the Vale of Joshua on the other side of the city, and the heathen Admiral of Spain had recalled his troops to prepare a hasty defense.

Not everyone in the heathen camp was pleased with that decision. King Brullant wore a stubborn look halfway between determination and despair. "I say again, Sire; those men in the Tower are like the serpent's tooth. Pluck out the fang and the snake will pose no threat."

"And for the final time I answer that I'll not send a thousand men against ten when an army waits in the other direction!"

King Sortibrant put a gentling hand on his friend's shoulder. "Brullant, our gods will surely aid us more if we oppose a Christian king than merely chase his men. It is They who decide matters in the end."

Brullant was defeated but unconvinced. "At least give me command of our rightmost wing, Sire. That shall place the Tower in my charge and let me ensure that the fang stays idle. Besides, I see some possibilities in the land..."

"You have my entire trust," said the Admiral. "Sortibrant, you shall command the left. Let us go and prepare."

THE FRENCH camp enjoyed considerably more order. The army waited for battle with the poise and excitement of a horse before the race. At last they would bring the enemy to grips! Only Charlemagne's heart bore a cloud. He summoned Fierabras to meet with him alone.

"My dear friend," said the King. "You know how well I've come to love you. It ill pleases me to think of harming your kin. For your sake I am willing to give your father the Admiral a final chance. If he will consent to be baptized, forsake his heathen gods, and agree to be Our friend, then I shall love him as I have come to love you. Not a penny of all his goods will I take, nor even an inch of land. But if he will not do these things, a battle cannot be avoided, and I can promise no mercy thereafter."

"Sir Emperor, if you send to my father a messenger bearing these terms then I shall be content. The sin will be on his own head if he denies you and I shall neither pray for nor give him any pity, even if I see him hewn and dead on the ground."

Charles turned to Dukes Reyner and Richard, who were at that time his chief counselors. "Who would you suggest to bear this message? My thought turns to Ganelon. He is well-spoken, a noble man, and you know how well he proved his prowess in the battle for Mantryble Bridge."

Duke Richard quickly agreed. "Truly Sire, Ganelon above all men would deliver your words in the tone and manner you'd like, with silver atop and iron beneath. But I mistrust this Admiral of Spain despite his being a good knight's father. 'Twould be a hazardous embassy to bear."

"I'll not command him," agreed the King. "We shall only ask." It turned out to be a moot debate. When Ganelon heard the mission described he immediately volunteered before the King could pose the question.

"Sire, your hope commands me as sternly as your words. I am your man entirely, in all things, and would willingly set my life in the hazard to see even your whim fulfilled. But in this matter there is Fierabras to consider as well.

"If these are the last words I speak in your court, let them be words of praise. Fierabras is a knight to admire and respect; valiant, honest, courageous, and true. What counts more to a man than family? What risk is too great to save and protect our kin? I would undertake this mission for his sake alone, even if you'd have preferred another."

Fierabras embraced him with teary eyes and kissed him on both cheeks. Ganelon returned his kind words and the pair left arm in arm. With Fierabras playing his squire, the knight was armed and ready within minutes. He rode off with a jaunty wave, his helm glittering on his head and his shield hung round his neck displaying the wheels of Mayence on a field of cherry red. His tall steed, Gascon, rose to a gallop and flew across the field.

Twenty Turks came out to meet him. He spoke proudly. "I bear a message from Charles the Great, King of the Franks and Emperor of the West. Lead me to your Admiral."

BALAN HELD court in a giant scarlet and purple pavilion, with his throne sitting on a platform that raised him above all heads. Ganelon stood before him with a lordly mien. One hand held Gascon's halter and the other gestured gracefully as he spoke.

"Saracen, take heed and understand that I am a messenger of Charles the Great, mighty King and Emperor of France. He sends word by me that if you forsake Mahon and your other diabolical gods and consent to be baptized in the One True Faith, he shall entirely spare your life, your lands, and your goods, along with those of your subjects and people. You shall also have His fullest love, and that of Fierabras, your son.

"A man who could sire so worthy a knight deserves to have this chance.

"But if you will not accept this offer, know that the Emperor shall defy you and bring you down, and with you your lands and subjects. You would be wiser in that case to flee than to fight, for if taken you would go to a dangerous death, your subjects would be dismembered, and your riches would be given to the King's servants. Take good counsel, therefore, before you give your answer."

The Admiral grew ever more angry as Ganelon's words went on, and by the end of this speech was so consumed with fury that he could only sputter. He pounded the arm of his throne in rage, then snatched up a stave and brandished it as if to strike the French messenger. "Wretch!" he finally spat. "Brigand! Your words condemn you. Charles can bear you but little love to send you to me thus. Your head will be my answer."

King Brullant stepped forward and cried, "Guards, seize him!"

Ganelon reacted before they could move. He swept his sword from its scabbard and struck Brullant through the chest. The Saracen king staggered and collapsed at his Admiral's feet.

As Sortibrant ran from the tent calling, "Guards! Guards!" Ganelon struck down two more men who sought to restrain him, leapt to his saddle, and then whirled away into the dawn. Thousands of Turks pursued the fleeing knight across the Vale of Joshua. He evaded them all, spurring his horse in a desperate push for freedom.

Up in the Tower Duke Naymon watched from a window. He called for Roland and Oliver. "My old eyes fail me. Who is that man that causes so great a tumult in the Saracens' camp?"

"A Christian to be sure," said Oliver, peering out. "It must be Ganelon. That would be my choice to bear a message if I were the Emperor Charles."

"God grant him safe deliverance," said Roland. "Look at him ride! That is a puissant man, make no mistake, and a knight who earns his fame."

Ganelon labored on against the insuperable odds, struggling through thousands of foes for the safety of Charlemagne's camp. Up in the Tower the knights crowded the windows and cheered lustily as he spurred back and forth like a hind fleeing the pack. Their voices dimmed for a moment when it seemed the enemy had caught him at last, surrounded on all sides at the top of a little hill; then roared with joy as he drew his sword Murgall and cut his way out. One man fell from a blow to the helm. A second he cleft through the breast. Then he came on Tenebres, the brother of king Sortibrant, and slew him too before breaking into the clear once again.

Roland and Oliver clutched each other and wept. "Oh valiant Baron!" cried Oliver. "May God preserve him brother, I love the man with all my heart. Save you and Charles, there's none I love any better. Would that I rode by his side – a great martyrdom would we make among these pagans!"

All Ganelon's feats made barely a dint in the numbers that pursued, however. The heathen closed in from all sides, howling like hungry wolves and eager for the kill. Ganelon made less and less progress with each sally. One after another, they cut off his lines of escape. Twenty men had circled him round with spears when the air began to shiver like the ocean before an angry storm. The Vale of Joshua shook and trembled to the sound of approaching thunder.

The foe scattered like hares, for Charlemagne had come in wrath.

GANELON knelt before the King to deliver the news of his embassy. Charles listened closely and immediately began to issue orders in a clear, crisp voice. "We shall advance in ten divisions. Richard and the Normans will lead the van. Reyner, you shall have the left. Ganelon, you take the right. Beware the hill on your flank. Aloys shall keep the fourth division to support your own."

After disposing the other troops he finished by saying, "I will command our reserve from the heights. I adjure you all to heed Our messengers, for the land is full of hills and vales and you'll have no sight beyond your own piece of the battle."

The news of Ganelon's deliverance reached the Admiral's tent at about the same time. It was met with considerably less aplomb.

King Sortibrant burst into tears, wailing and brandishing his sword. "You have slain my brother, Charles. For that I will have your head!"

This vow greatly pleased the Admiral. He laughed as Sortibrant hacked the silk hangings to shreds.

Sortibrant was still raging when word arrived that the Emperor Charles had begun his assault. The Admiral embraced his councilor and said, "Take a hundred thousand men and meet the French on the field. I will hold a like amount in reserve. But if you come upon Charles or Fierabras, slay them not. Bring them to me instead."

Brullant was missed already.

THE ARMIES met before the Vale of Joshua with a gigantic clash that shook the stones of Aygremore's walls. The French trumpets sounded high and clear above the fray, commanding men to shift this way and that within the swirling confusion of the battle. The Saracens also surged forward, but lacking the same discipline, were far less effective. Thousands milled around looking for someone to fight or else waiting to be told where to go. This quickly yielded an advantage to the attacking French despite the Saracens having some tens of thousands more in numbers. But it was a great battle nevertheless, and all men know how many things depend on chance when swords and spears take command of the day. And, of course, the Admiral lay in reserve with an army larger than either already on the field.

At one point Sortibrant came with twenty thousand men near to where Charlemagne gave commands. "Where is the Emperor Charles?" he cried. "Where is the Bandit King? You were a fool to ever cross into Spain. You'll have no time to repent it though, for this day your life will end. Come and face me, you dotard!"

The Saracen's words inflamed the King's heart with rage. He lowered his long spear and charged. The defiant heathen rode to meet him.

Charlemagne's point took Sortibrant on the shield with such force that sundry bits of his armor flew high in the air and the Saracen sagged in the saddle, stunned and confused. He never had a chance to recover.

The Emperor drew his great sword Joyeuse and struck over and over until his enemy fell dead on the earth.

Meanwhile, at the center of the lines a Turkish chieftain named Coldroe stormed through the French troops, slaying many fair men. He shattered the shield of Sir Jehan de Bretagne, then smote him through the body. He likewise robbed the lives of the good Earls Huon and Guernyer of Milan, and set a great pall of fear on the French who stood before him. With a sneer he rose in his stirrups and cried out, "Weak and helpless I name you all! Who is the next that wants to die?"

Richard of Normandy commanded that part of the line. He drew his sword and answered that challenge with a wordless fury. Coldroe met him with a heavy blow to the shield. Richard rocked back to avoid its force. This threw the Saracen so off balance that a little tug by Richard almost tumbled him from his seat. Coldroe dropped his shield hand in a desperate grab at his saddle. He might have been better off on the ground.

As Coldroe struggled to recover his balance, Richard raised his blade and gave a subtle command that caused his horse to rear. When Coldroe sat up, the steed came down, and with that weight came Richard's sword. The combination cost this Turk his boastful head.

On the far right of the field Ganelon and his troops made a great slaughter among the enemy. Fierabras rode at his side and personally accounted for more than fifty men. The Saracens broke before them like still water being cut by the prow of a mighty ship. They were on the brink of rout when fortune struck a blow in the heathens' favor.

A crossbow bolt flew out of nowhere and crashed on Fierabras' helm with a resounding *clang!* louder than any church bell. The giant knight sagged and would have slipped among the gnashing hooves had Ganelon not caught his reins and brought him back to safety. The enemy managed to stiffen and re-form with the two French champions gone, but when Fierabras recovered a few minutes later, the tide once again began to favor the French. Steadily, consistently, more and more of the heathens began to weigh his chance of escape. Their eyes evaluated the rear as much as they did to the front.

By this combination of discipline, organization and valor the French slowly began to dominate the field. Admiral Balan saw the balance shifting and deemed the time ripe to advance with the hundred thousand fresh troops he'd held in reserve. Charlemagne committed the last of his meager reserves as well and rode to battle at their head. That made the odds a bit more than two to one.

UP IN THE Tower, the imprisoned paladins watched the field in bitter frustration as good men fought and died. The battle had slowed to the pace of two monstrous beasts locked in a death grip. One was larger, stronger and heavier; the other nobler, braver and better skilled. Whichever gave ground first would pay the ultimate price. They longed to help, but five thousand Saracens guarded the door and pinned their band in place.

The Admiral was the mightiest of all the Saracen knights despite his faults. His arrival on the field made devastating inroads among the French. He slew by the dozens and the French lines trembled before him. Afire with the chance of victory, Balan waved his bloody sword over his head and cried, "To me! Men of Mahon, ride to me now! Great rewards will I give to those who help me to finish this adventure!"

That cry was his undoing. Consumed with visions of promised gold, the guards around the Tower abandoned their watch and hurried to respond.

Roland had been grinding his teeth and banging his fist on the stone sill of the window when the force of jailers rode off. "Look there!" he cried to his fellows. They gathered by the window, unbelieving.

The thought arrived to all of them at about the same time, but as usual it was Duke Naymon who gave it voice. "There are horses free on the field. Let us partake of the plenty."

THE FINAL Saracen reserves, twenty thousand men of the city militia, cheered lustily as their Admiral led the way to victory. His puissance could not be stopped. They danced with joy as the French trembled and broke before him.

Then death arrived from behind.

The fiends from the Tower were free! And at their head was the devil incarnate, the one called Roland who wore the red and white. Heads flew up around him like quail fleeing from a monstrous hound. At his side the other demons took nearly as heavy a toll, cutting down men like a mower's scythe. Horrified to senseless panic, the militia fled.

Fortune had favored the heathen once. Now she turned her face. The paladins had come from behind, so the reserves went forward to escape. Twenty thousand shrieking, panicked men poured squarely into the rear of the Saracen lines. Their fear spread like flames in a room of hay, with the charging knights a burning coal at the heart.

The Admiral quickly realized that the battle would be lost if he didn't succeed in a desperate chance. *'If Charlemagne dies,'* he said to himself, *'the foe will crumble. He is the head of the snake.'* He circled the knots of fighting men until the King's standard, the Oriflamme, rose before him. *'Perfect!'* The Admiral covered himself with the cloak of a fallen French knight and crept closer, to a spot directly behind the King.

The knights from the Tower had likewise spotted the Oriflamme. Naymon, Ogier and Thierry split off to bring news of their release to the Emperor, while the younger knights continued to wreak their unique brand of havoc. Charles waved jubilantly to the oncoming barons, his attention completely focused on the joy of seeing them alive. It was Ogier who saw the giant knight in a French cloak rear up behind the King and prepare a treacherous stroke.

The noble Dane spurred his horse forward and leapt headfirst from the saddle. All seven feet of him flew past the King and drove the threat to the ground. Enraged by what he thought to be treason, Ogier ripped the helm off the man beneath him and struck him unconscious with an angry blow from his armored fist. It was only then that he realized who he'd tackled and felled.

The Saracens knew immediately, however. The last of their courage collapsed with the fall of the Admiral. Shaky lines dissolved into a disorganized mass of frightened men. All that remained was the harvest.

WHEN FIERABRAS and Ganelon broke through the foe a few minutes later, they found the battle all but done, and the King embracing his nephew with tears of joy. "Roland," he cried, "you have saved us yet again! Without you our valor is as naught."

"So that is Roland," said Fierabras a little wistfully. "He doesn't look half so fierce as rumor would make him seem. I regret that we'll have no chance to cross swords in honorable combat."

Ganelon shook his head. "Say not so. You are my friend and I prefer my friends with their shoulders, necks, and heads all firmly connected."

When Fierabras gave him an odd look, Ganelon continued. "Roland is like the arm of fate. No man could face him and hope to live. Not even you. Nor any ten men. Nor tens of tens. No one will ever slay Roland but Roland himself. I suppose that might be contrived, but the plan would take some thought..."

Fierabras began to reply, but the arrival of another rider diverted his attention. "Look! It's Oliver!" He set spurs to his horse and bounded ahead.

As Ganelon shook his head again, this time merely bemused, his cousin Aloys rode up to take Fierabras' place at his side. "Well your Grace – You have once again managed to almost win the prize. This morning you were the toast of France. Now you're just another moon to Roland's sun."

"Say not so," said Ganelon. "He earns his fame."

"And you do not? Roland's glory blinds the King to all others. What reward will you have for the day's work? A hearty 'Well done' and the chance to do it again?"

Aloys backed away as Ganelon's face turned angry. "Be that as it may," the younger man said. "If I want even that much reward I'd best go harvest a few heads of my own. There's still some fighting to do, you know. Will you join me?"

Ganelon pulled on his helmet, drew his bloody sword, and spurred toward the last few pockets of resistance without a word. Aloys laughed and followed.

Thus the day was won and the first great conquest of Spain begun.

BISHOP TURPIN took charge of the relics. There in front of the collected army he displayed their marvelous properties to one and all. The air was filled for days with the glorious scent they exuded.

Only the Admiral seemed unimpressed with this miracle. Despite numerous chances and a sermon from the King's own lips, he stayed resolved to his heathen gods. Indeed he spat in the font prepared for his baptism, and would have murdered the bishop with his own hands had Ogier not intervened. Finally even Fierabras had to admit the man was beyond redemption. The King had him beheaded, together with everyone else in the city who would not convert.

Charles set Guy of Burgundy into the Admiral's place, newly wed to the beautiful Floripas. They ruled Aygremore together long and well.

Fierabras also received vast estates. These he held from Guy, though more in name than substance. Over the years the brothers by marriage grew closer than many tied by blood.

As for the wealth of the Admiral's treasury, this was distributed among the army with Charlemagne's customary wisdom and generosity. Not a man went back to France with less in his pouch than would buy a dozen acres of land.

All of this took the rest of the summer to settle, and the harvest had almost arrived when the last farewells were made. Cheers filled the air as Charles the Great, King of France and Emperor of the West, savored the scent of triumph and rode toward home with all twelve Peers at his side.

THUS ENDED the great events of the year. But there was one smaller event that deserves to be told.

The chronicles relate that King Charles found himself much taken with the wondrous manner in which the relics would float in the air. He selected two of the smallest pieces and secreted them in each forefinger of his gloves. Throughout the long ride home he would delight in a game that went like this: first he'd strike up a casual conversation with some unwitting soul. Then he would remove a glove from hand and leave it to hang in midair before the stunned man's eyes. And then he would roar with laughter at expressions and antics to follow.

Nothing Bishop Turpin said could defeat his joy in this game, until a day arrived that one of the gloves slipped away by accident as the king rode by on a forest trail. A common man – most say a baker – followed that same path a few minutes later and ran face first into the floating glove. Neither his expression nor his antics have been told, but being a right good and pious man, the victim thereafter took the glove to Bishop Turpin who displayed it after mass to the King. Then Charlemagne's friend and confessor imposed on him this penance: First, that the baker, having received a buffet from the hand of the King, must be named a knight and given such lands as were needed to support his new station. Second, that the King must cease his little game, "which smacks not a little of blasphemy." And finally that all the relics must be returned to Rome to be held forever by the Pope.

To all of these things the King agreed. And from that day to this, the land of France has held its bakers in more esteem than any other nation on earth.

THE END

AFTERWORD

A word on my sources.

Everything from the encounter between Oliver and Fierabras on was adapted from William Caxton's 1485 translation of the 13th century text *Speculum Historiale*. The one remaining copy of Caxton's work, a folio volume with 96 leaves, is kept in the King's Library of the British Museum, Press–mark C. 10 *b*. 9. My source is the 1880–1881 copy published in the Early English Text Society Extra Series (xxxvi – xxxvii) under the title *Lyf of the Noble and Crysten Prynce Charles the Grete* (reprinted as one volume 1967). The editor's notes to the Caxton text indicate that two copies of the *Speculum Historiale* remain in existence. Caxton apparently did a fairly close translation.

A different author/translator told a somewhat less readable version of the same story that was published under the title *Sir Ferumbras* in volume xxxiv of the EETS Extra Series. A third version, and my main source for the early chapters on the Battle of Rome, came from the book *Three Middle English Charlemagne Romances*, edited by Alan Lupack (Medieval Institute Publications, 1990), and particularly the part enti-tled *"The Romance of the Sowdone of Babylone and of Fierabras His Soon Who Conquered Rome."* Finally, I can also recommend Alfred J. Church's very readable version in *Stories Of Charlemagne And The Twelve Peers Of France (From The Old Romances)*, pp. 127–229 (The Macmillan Company, 1902).

The fight between Roland and Mambrino – normally named "Fer-ragus" or "Ferragut" is a classic found in so many variations it would be hard to list them. *Bullfinch's Mythology* is a good place to start.

If you're interested to see how much I changed (and it was a lot), these are the places to look. I encourage you to try. I embarked on this project with a terrible fear that I'd be forced to more or less learn a whole new language. After all, Caxton predates Shakespeare by a hundred years. What a pleasure to find I was wrong! Caxton's English is surprisingly easy to penetrate. I urge you to give it a try. Here's a hint for the trouble spots: when in doubt, try reading the section aloud with an over-the-top English accent. It may sound silly but it really works.

In any case, and despite my paean to "adaptation," in many parts the language was clear enough that several sections that needed no significant changes. There were even instances where I could even lift some turns of phrase and make real efforts to incorporate the author's style. Consider it a challenge: Can spot you where it's the original author being corny versus the times when I'm the one to blame? The only phrase you won't have to wonder about is this: *"If I'm to be civil to a Christian king, I must first slake my thirst for Christian blood!"* Caxton gets all the credit for that one.

A more pervasive change came from the simple evolution of written English over the past 600 years. The unknown author of the *Speculum Historiale* was transcribing an oral tale; *i.e.,* he told the story out loud and then wrote down what he said. Caxton did the same thing. In both cases, this was the norm for the age. That norm has changed.

Written English now differs from the spoken in several important ways, and reading the oral version is jarring to say the least. To the limits of my skill, and subject to a few exceptions, I've transformed the story to fit our literary conventions with a few archaic terms and constructions to keep an "antique" feel.

CHAPTER NOTES

> *SPOILER ALERT:*
>
> *Do not read ahead. The following notes give away various parts of the story. Some of them spoil future chapters too. You have been warned.*

CHAPTER 1 – THE INVASION OF ROME

<u>King Iblis of Samarkand.</u> The original called him "King Lucifer of Baghdad." Why the change? There were two main reasons.

First, "Lucifer" was a bit too heavy handed even for me. Okay, I get it: Balan is allied with the Devil himself. But giving a character that name takes away the human drama and the possibility that he might be something less than evil incarnate. "Iblis" is the Arab equivalent to Lucifer so I used that instead. It's no better in the abstract, but at least has enough subtlety to get missed by people who don't read the chapter notes at the back of the book.

His realm was changed to Samarkand because Balan is often described as the "Sultan of Baghdad." Sultan and King were probably enough to distinguish the two but why take the risk? Besides, it let me throw in another of those Silk Road names that sound so exotic.

<u>Who is to blame for this war?</u> In a word, no one. Our view of war is very different from that of our ancestors. Modern weapons and the horrors of World War I changed everything. For the original authors of these stories, war was an everyday, normal, and usually admirable endeavor that brought honor to all who were involved. Kings and knights didn't want peace and plenty. They wanted war. That was their *raison d'etre*.

Thus the original makes no particular effort to pin the blame for this war on either side – because the authors didn't see any "blame" in the first place. Rome allowed pirates to raid the "heathen" ships because that's what you did. What other purpose do Saracens have than to act as a source of ready plunder? The Sultan responded by trying to level the city because that's what Christians are for – to be killed and enslaved by Saracens. Right and wrong matter a lot, but they are 100% defined by which side of the fence you're on.

From the storyteller's point of view, all that matters is the scale. This isn't going to be just another war. It's going to be a really, really big war!

Wow. Those armies are huge... Let's be entirely clear about this: The number of men described in all of the armies is so vastly overstated that it doesn't come within laughing range of the most extreme guesses at what might be possible.

The numbers described for Charlemagne's army exceed the population – men, women, and children – of medieval Paris and medieval London *combined*. The Saracen numbers are at least twice that high. If your B.S. button didn't get pushed, you need to find a new one! The simple logistics to keep such numbers fed, clothed and mobile were inconceivable for any medieval state.

So why not change the numbers to something more realistic? Wouldn't it be simpler to divide everything by a hundred? I thought about that enough to give it a try. The result was terrible.

At its core this story is a medieval fantasy about the greatest armies in the world meeting in a titanic clash of opposing heroes – with "ours" coming out on top, of course. Realistic numbers take away from that sense of over-the-top fantasy.

In addition, there's a constant thread to the effect that *'back in the Good Old Days everything was bigger and better.'* Progress is a fairly modern idea. People tended to believe the opposite when these stories were written, that the world was slowly spinning downward and could only be saved by moving backwards toward a lost golden age. There are a lot of politicians who play that card even today, and even though we *know* that both life and politics were at least as ugly back in the "good old days," with a whole lot less in the way of creature comforts and leisure time to balance the ugliness out. In any case, the story is built on the idea that things were bigger, shinier, and grander back in the days of Charles the Great, and the inconceivable size of the armies is part of what gets that across.

Third, there is no consistency in the scope of the exaggeration. In one case it might make sense to cut the numbers to a tenth or a hundredth, but others might call for anything from a half to a factor of a thousand. It has no reason. Oddly enough, however, if does have a sort of rhythm and rhyme. A cast of thousands means *"a significant tactical unit."* Tens of thousands means, *"Aren't you impressed? That's way more soldiers than any of our kings could even dream of getting together!"* And hundreds of thousands is a signal for, *"This is the stuff of legends!"*

Floripas? Where'd the girl come from? You can't have romance without beautiful maidens! What's wrong with you? Just keep an eye on this one. If you're expecting a lily-cheeked flower just waiting for her menfolk to decide her fate, you'll get the first part – the lovely complexion – but the rest could upset your preconceptions. This is not a modern overlay either. The Floripas you see is the Floripas you get even if you go back to the original sources.

Duke Hernaut and his son Aimery. The original name was "Savaris". I originally changed it to avoid potential confusion with the word "Saracen," but then realized that the character needed a bit more depth if I was going to "show" the siege of Rome in a modern way instead of just "telling" what happened in violation of the Author's Secret Code. Hernaut is actually a known character from a whole series of other stories in the Carolingian Cycle: one of the four sons of the legendary Garin de Monglane, father of a hero named Aimery of Narbonne (who has his own famous poem) and grandfather of Guilluame d'Orange (for whom William of Orange was later named, no doubt). Even better, the Hernaut character from those stories was the brother of Oliver's father Duke Reyner, which makes Oliver and Aimery first cousins and thereby ties the front part of the book to the back part just a little better.

Consider the appearance of Hernaut and Aimery as a gift/cameo for true fans of the Matter of France. And this whole discussion as a gift for the sort of people who are always dying to know how the author's mind was working as the story got written.

The Siege of Rome scenes were added as a prequel to the Invasion of Spain parts that I'd written several years before. This worked better if I consciously enhanced the Duke's importance to make him the Christian viewpoint character. Giving him a son worked even better. Then, once that was done, I went back to my research and (re)discovered Hernaut and Aimery. A perfect fit! The edits were made and yielded what's now in your hand.

CHAPTER 2 – THE SARACEN ASSAULT

The original versions were a mess. There's no other way to put it. I have zero doubt that this is why Caxton chose to start his vastly more coherent tale with the duel between Oliver and Fierabras that is now my Chapter 7. So at least 90% of these early chapters is original work on my part – in the sense that I took the basic plot and then wrote something to fit. Hopefully I did it without changing the look and feel too much.

The basic goal of Chapter 2 is to set up the rest of the book. The Saracens are cruel, somewhat competent, and led by an array of very impressive champions. Courage and brilliance can slow them down but nothing short of Charlemagne could possibly hope to fight them on an equal footing. Unfortunately, the Romans are just a bit too proud to bend their necks and that's going to cause trouble.

The authors are French, you see. The audience is French too. All would be good if the rest of Europe – especially the Pope – would bow down humbly to the King of France and acknowledge His ultimate greatness. But, alas, those silly foreigners didn't know what was good for them even back in the Good Old Days.

CHAPTER 3 – THE SIEGE OF ROME

The originals are just as confused about the siege of Rome as they are for the initial attack. Especially when it comes to describing who did what and when they did it in relation to everything else that's going on.

I added a number of scenes to bring some continuity, and re-framed most of the others to fit them into that larger picture. In particular, I completely invented the landscape and defenses around the city in an effort to come up with some way to have (a) the scene where Hernaut gets trapped outside the only working gate by Iblis' trick , (b) the scene where Astrogot smashes the still-defended gate only to get killed by the portcullis, and (c) the scene where the Saracens get into the city via the efforts of a traitor, whom Fierabras then beheads. Why would the city of Rome have only one gate, and how could it be taken three separate times in three separate ways?

For that matter, what kind of defenses could make them look at those numbers outside their walls and then make the decision to wait until a "more convenient time" to send for Charlemagne's help? I hope you liked my solution. It's meant to be a combination of magnificent and scenic fantasy with semi-plausible decision making.

It is emphatically *not* an attempt to portray the city of Rome as it is, was, or was ever really imagined. For that matter, I should admit that the giant moat in Chapter 2 owes as much to *Leiningen Versus the Ants* as it does to either *The Sowdayne of Babylon* or Caxton's *Lyf of Charles the Grete*. Just like the other revamped defenses, it was created to give some kind of rational frame story that would allow for most of the existing combat scenes that the originals dealt with more clearly.

One scene got deleted. It centered on a sally organized and led by the Pope:

> *The Pope then summoned all the people of the city to Saint Peter's, and thither went every man. He said on high, "My dear children, You know well how matters lie; against the Saracens*

that now be here We may not long endure. They break our walls and our towers all with casts of their engines. Therefore you here shall give me counsel. The enemy has withdrawn to his host, and laid down his arms for the nonce. Therefore, I think, I might be best to fall on them early tomorrow. We have thirty thousand men; twenty thousand shall go with me, and in this city ten shall stay to govern the community."

The senators assented immediately saying, "Better might no man say. Let it be done with the coming of dawn, And God bring them home again."

The Pope displayed the high banner of Rome, and he absolved every man through gracious God from his judgment seat. He prayed to Saint Peter and to Paul for help and succor, and also to Our Lady, that sweet flower, to save the city of Rome from woe...

The sally failed because Fierabras was too alert. He saw the Romans coming, blew a brass horn to wake the camp and then organized a sturdy defense. The Romans were forced to retreat after absorbing another round of enormous loss.

I spent a good bit of heartbreak debating both sides but finally concluded that the scene was little more than a carbon copy of the earlier battles. It added length without advancing the story, and therefore had to go.

St. Peters. Yes, it did exist at the time. St. Peter's Basilica was built by the Emperor Constantine (beginning c. 324) and completed by his son Constantius (in c. 354). Tradition says it was built over the grave of Peter the Apostle.

CHAPTER 4 – A LADY'S FAVOR

This entire chapter is new, and is another example of something I wrote to fill a gaping chasm or two in the sources. In particular, Caxton's *Lyf of Charles the Grete* specifically says that (a) Fierabras killed the Pope and Rome, (b) Duke Richard of Normandy killed the Admiral's Uncle Corsuble during the battles at Rome, and (c) Floripas fell in love with Guy of Burgundy by seeing him over the castle walls. The *Sultan of Babylon* is equally specific that (d) Balan and all his men were gone from Rome by the time that Charlemagne arrived.

This chapter was created to bridge those gaps. I hope you liked it.

And yes, the word "boulevard" was used correctly. This is one of my favorite word origins. "Boulevard" originally referred to the walls around a city. The word derives from the same root as "bulwark", meaning "barrier" or "fortification." The opposite meaning – a wide city street – arose after such walls came down in the 19th century. Remember that cities had grown up organically, over time, and that real estate developers in olden days were just as rapacious as the ones we know today. In places like Paris the older streets hardly deserved the name. To our eyes they would have seemed more like alleys and lanes winding away in the spaces between buildings. When the city walls came down, however, it left wide, empty rings that went all the way around the central parts of the city. These were a godsend to travelers and traders alike, and quickly became arteries that even the greediest developer could not assail.

CHAPTER 5 – CHECKED BY THE GIANT MAMBRINO

The giant in this adventure is more properly named Ferragus, Ferracutus, or any of a dozen similar names. I've changed it to avoid confusion with Fierabras, who has a more central role in the rest of the story. Why "Mambrino" instead? Glad you asked!

The famous romance *Orlando Furioso* features a helmet originally owned by a moor named King Mambrino, which made its wearer invulnerable. The parallels were too good to ignore. Cervantes played off this idea too, so I'm in good company. There's a famous scene where Don Quixote places a barber's bowl on his head, all the while insisting that it was Mambrino's enchanted helm. The musical *Man of La Mancha* devotes a song to it:

Golden helmet of Mambrino
There can be no hat like thee.
Thee and I now, ere I die now
Will make golden history...

The battle between Roland and the giant is one of the most popular adventures of the Carolingian cycle. It doesn't appear in any of the specific sources that drove most of this tale, but it fit the timeline so perfectly that I decided to add it in. In particular, it gave me a clean way to bridge the timeframe between the Admiral's invasion of Italy and Charlemagne's revenge attack on Spain. The sources would have you believe it all happened in a single year. When you write it out, however, that's clearly impossible.

The specifics of this adventure vary greatly but a few essentials are always there. First, the giant's main asset is an invulnerable hide. And second, his style of fighting is to grab his foe and carry him away kicking to prison. Most versions characterize the giant as either a devil in human form or the Ultimate Heathen Warrior. Neither approach fit this situation because I've chosen to downplay the religious elements, and Fierabras has occupied the latter role.

There are also versions where the character I'm calling Mambrino is described as the gatekeeper for Morgan Le Fey, the wicked fairy queen who appears as a running villain throughout the Carolingian cycle. This version featured an exchange I particularly liked that occurs between Roland and Mambrino during the break in their bout. The giant offers a compromise – if Roland will walk away, he will give his prisoners to the Fairy instead of condemning them to a more brutal fate. Why fight so hard to prevent your friends from living out their lives in pampered luxury? It's an added temptation for Roland to refuse. I thought long and hard about that using this version of the story but finally decided that it would violate the rule against mentioning main characters who don't appear in the story at hand.

That pushed me toward a dark version of the Magic Northern Giant who appears in so many fairy tales. This is why Mambrino speaks like he's not all there – it fits the motif and grants credibility to the prodigies of strength. Carolingian giants are rarely that dim, though there are exceptions.

For what it's worth, I adore this description of Ogier the Dane.

> *In sheer physical stature he was by far the grandest of Charlemagne's knights. Agile, graceful and incredibly strong, he also stood a full seven feet tall and weighed more than 300 pounds.*

This is an accurate physical description of the Ogier from the tales, though he actually wouldn't have claimed any allegiance to Northern ways. Ogier was given to Charlemagne as a hostage at age 9 or so and always felt more French than Danish (a client kingdom). Moreover, the Danes were not of Viking stock — they were its victims according to the sagas. So the axe is probably not technically appropriate either. I made all these changes so Mambrino would have defeated a variety of physical challenges before facing Roland: the mounted Duke Basyn, the powerful Ogier and the swift and skillful Oliver. These add up to make Mambrino "Bad Juju" and add to the vague something extra that makes Roland the greatest knight of all.

CHAPTER 6 – ASSAULT INTO SPAIN

I moved this into a new year, but other than that it's mostly part of the original story. There, Charlemagne sailed his army (of 300,000 men!) from Rome to Aygremore, where he overwhelmed a castle that guarded the way into Spain. And then slaughtered everything he could find.

I moved that into a march over the mountains because the B.S. button was getting pushed harder than even I could bear, and I feared that the same thing would happen to you. Besides, it made more sense for later scenes that require the army to cross the river at Mantryble. If Charles has such a great fleet ready to hand, why not simply bypass the fortress?

What I did *not* change was how the Christians behaved when they got the upper hand. I repeat: what we think of as the "horrors of war" carried no such connotation for the authors of medieval romance, and there was no such thing as a universal view of right and wrong that applied without regard to who you were. It was "wrong" for the Admiral to kill and enslave the population of Rome because he is a Saracen and his victims were civilian good guys. It is "right" for Charlemagne to do exactly the same thing because he is a Christian and his victims are civilian bad guys.

The fact that women and children were dying in their homes wasn't particularly noteworthy in and of itself. Life was cheap and people died all the time.

Why is Tuesday sacred to the god of war? Tuesday is the day of Tiu, the Germanic war god, identified with Mars. The Latin name for Tuesday, 'dies Martis' (which survives in the French 'mardi') attests to the longstanding association of Tuesday with Mars.

CHAPTER 7 – OLIVER AND FIERABRAS

An ongoing theme – it's all about the champions. Champions are a staple theme of the Carolingian cycle. This is one of the things you, the audience, needs to understand going in. Charlemagne wins because his paladins are all but invincible. He loses in the end when three are lost at a stroke during the Battle of Roncesvalles: Roland and Oliver to their deaths, and Ganelon to his own treason. Things are never the same after that.

Here we see the Admiral of Spain losing his champions one by one. The audience knows where that's going to lead! First came the fall of Astrogot during the siege of Rome. Next the fall of Corsuble in the ill-fated attempt to trap a few paladins. Then the invulnerable Mambrino met his end. And now we see the Admiral lose his greatest champion of all – his own son – in the worst possible way, because he adds his strength to the Christian cause.

And then there's the twist. Charlemagne, in one of those seemingly irrational moments that only turn out well with hindsight, gives the advantage back to the Admiral with all sorts of bonus extras. Has the

Emperor of France pissed away the entire war with his impulsive act? It looks that way... But maybe not.

Right there you have the entire story arc in a nutshell.

As for the adventure in this particular chapter, the twin battles of Roland v. Ferragus/Mambrino, and of Oliver v. Fierabras are THE prototype "knight-versus-giant" stories. You think that's an old cliché? It may be, but these two scenes are where it started.

I knew a lady once who rolled her eyes at a line in *Hamlet*:

"Listen to this! *'To be or not to be.'* How corny can you get?"

What can you say? At one level she's right. It is corny, because everyone's heard that line so many thousands of times that no modern writer could dream of using it except as a quote or a bit of dialogue. But at a deeper level she was 100% wrong, because *Hamlet* is where that line began. The same is true of these two battles between Charlemagne's greatest knights and these two classic versions of the invincible giant.

I have read any number of variations on the Oliver and Fierabras fight in particular. They're pretty much all a lot of fun. If you feel like taking an excursion into original sources that is one little side path I can recommend. Interestingly enough, and at least one scholarly source I read used the presence or absence of Fierabras as a tool to categorize the larger threads of the Charlemagne epic. [My apologies, but I can't remember the cite.] The bottom line is this: If your ancestors hail from Western Europe, this was a story they knew and loved growing up.

CHAPTER 8 – CAPTURES AND RESCUES

Note how hard it is to get a fix on Charlemagne's character – particularly looking back. He's a man of such incredible extremes that he's very hard to judge. Naymon is the first one he asks for advice, of course; the unusual thing is that he refused to listen. At first this seems like a blatant, emotion-driven mistake. The King himself seems to think so later on, but once his word's been given he can't turn back. And yet – had the King not been so foolish and headstrong, would they ever have rescued Oliver at all? Was this the hand of Providence at work through its chosen tool? Nothing is ever clear about Charlemagne.

It's also worth looking at the parallels between the two Kings. They send essentially identical messages! What a fascinating non-coincidence.

Their contrasts are interesting too. Charlemagne may be headstrong, but he rules by love and respect. The Admiral, foams, spits, turns colors, and rules by rage and intimidation.

As the chapter progresses, other characters emerge, Duke Naymon in particular. He has a sparkling wit if you look for it. One of my favorite lines in the entire book is Naymon's off-hand comment to Galafer:

> *"We found twenty scoundrels on the field who would*
> *have taken our horses. God be thanked, they paid for*
> *this a heavy price."*

Think about that for a moment. Naymon just called Balan's twenty dead vassals a pack of horse thieves. That particular insult probably carried about the same weight in Medieval times as it did in the Old West. This is an example of the Duke's famous cleverness; his words can sound almost innocent to a bystander while at the same time delivering a deadly insult to the one who hears the message.

His wit goes beyond mere words, too. He thinks their way past the bridge warden, Galafer, despite everything Roland does to make that almost impossible. (What a clever way to get rid of those heads). But he's not soft; when they arrive at Aygremore he puts his words in the Admiral's ear as sharply as a dirk, and when he "plays at the coal" with Iblis in Chapter 9, he hits the man so hard that his eyes pop out and roll around the floor.

Floripas and the Misogyny that Wasn't. During this chapter, three or four separate people repeat the same line:

> *"You should not trust such tasks to a woman. They are changeable, inconstant, and not to be trusted in such affairs. Just think of all the men who have been led astray by the doings of women."*

Every time it's said, the man ignores the message and the woman (Floripas) does exactly the opposite of what that man expected. At least one of the scholarly texts I've read characterized this as an example of "medieval misogyny." You want my opinion? Bunk.

I'm a storyteller, not a scholar. In that capacity I can tell you that whenever you see a repeating line, it's going to be either an oral sing-along for the crowd, or something that's meant as a joke. Having studied it now in some detail, I'm morally certain that this particular line was meant to make you laugh.

Every one of the men who quoted that line was a Saracen; *i.e.,* a bad guy. It started with Iblis (a/k/a Lucifer) back in Chapter 3. Another was a jailer who promptly got brained with his own keys in a classic and famous example of medieval humor (one gets the feeling that dungeon guards weren't very popular.) By contrast, the good guys do *not* say such things. To the contrary, they treat Floripas as if she were made of gold. And far from betraying the people who treat her well, she's directly responsible for saving their lives in half a dozen different spots – most of which required a quick wit and steady head under pressure. How can you call that an example of a "boy's story that teaches disdain for the girls?"

One could argue that Floripas' secret devotion to a Christian knight is an example of "female treachery," but not with real success. The woman who falls helplessly in love at first sight (with a hero, of course) is nothing more than a stereotype. It's not particularly complimentary, but neither is the one about the man who glimpses a bit of hair from afar and spends the next twelve years on a tortuous quest to earn a pat on the head.

How did the scholars miss what I think is so patently plain? In my opinion, it's because they're scholars rather than performers. If you only look at the words on the page, something like this could easily slip past. When you're looking to *tell* the story, however – to perform it in the same spirit as your counterpart would have done a thousand years ago – something extra comes to the table. It's not so much that you see new truths, as you see what's there in a different light.

Do I know this story better than the experts who wrote those books? Not a chance. But I do know it in a different way, and every once in a while that angle can reveal a wonderful truth the experts may have missed.

CHAPTER 9 – THE TOWER

This chapter is mainly about Floripas. Even the famous scene where Naymon "plays at the coal" with Iblis revolves around her in one way or another. I can just see her leaning close to Roland, batting her beautiful eyelashes and saying, *"That horrible man has hurt my feelings so much. Can big, strong you think of some way to make him stop?"* Flutter, flutter, snicker-snack.

But she's not all fluff and manipulation. Far from it. It's Floripas who defeats the Enchanter, and Floripas who devises the strategy of hurling coin as a defense. That threat creates the stalemate that later allows the Paladins to be saved. Similar achievements appear later on.

The other character who begins to emerge is King Brullant. Sortibrant actually believes in his gods, but Brullant's the one we're learning to fear. A heathen, yes, but a practical one. Could he be the next coming of Corsuble?

CHAPTER 10 – THE RIDE OF RICHARD OF NORMANDY

This is another famous scene. I fidgeted with it to enhance the sense of Richard as a riding expert, but the main change was the shift from a magic steed to a magic saddle.

In Caxton's work, Coldroe rode a horse with the tail of a peacock, the rump of a partridge, a tiny head, and a coat that was fiery red on one side and "white as a fleur de lis" on the other. I gather that medieval audiences loved that sort of thing, but it jangles against the modern taste. I thought about changing it to a hippogriff or griffin, but both of those can fly, which would ruin the scene, and magic items are familiar enough to slide seamlessly into our fictive dream. I can't be sure, but it wouldn't surprise me if the saddle would jar the medieval mind as much as the feathered horse would have done to us.

Please note that the white hart was a common literary symbol. I'm told that it represents supernatural forces at play, in this case the hand of Providence. A medieval audience would have immediately understood that the scene shows an actual miracle in progress.

It's also worth noting the horns of Ganelon's dilemma in both this Chapter and the next one. He's caught between his family ties and his loyalty to the King.

CHAPTER 11 – THE BATTLE OF MANTRYBLE BRIDGE
and CHAPTER 12 – THE FINAL ASSAULT

Ogier's view of how to die is an eerie echo of how Oliver actually went in the *Song of Roland*.

> *"When I go, my sword shall be in my hand, and the heap of pagan dead shall be so high that men will marvel forever!"*

CHAPTER 13 – THE BATTLE OF AYGREMORE

The story can stand by itself here. What needs to be said was discussed above or expanded down below, in the discussion of the *Song of Roland*. I must admit, however, to cutting more out of the story at this point than in anywhere else.

Caxton included a long scene in which Admiral Balan refused to convert despite the best the French can do. Charlemagne delivered a whole sermon, and Fierabras begged him to submit in several ways.

(Floripas would rather they stopped wasting time and kill him, which earns a rebuke from her brother). In fear for his life, Balan finally agreed to be stripped and brought to the font for baptism, but at the end he reneged and tries to drown the bishop. That was the final straw.

Then comes the scene where Floripas strips to be baptized. Caxton describes this picture with loving detail: suffice it to say that she made a lot of friends on her trip to the font, and Guy got a lot of envious stares.

Caxton ends his story with the recovery of the relics. After some months Charlemagne asks Floripas to turn them over, which she does. Bishop Turpin tests them before the whole army and proves their authenticity by the fact that they float in midair. Caxton makes a number of pointed editorial asides about how many purported relics turn out to be frauds, which I moved to Chapter 9 for the sake of flow.

The last scene with the glove also appears in the original, at least in part. I added the baker and his legacy. Sometimes you need to end on a smile. Fare thee well my friends, and thank you for joining me on this joyous trip through time!

ABOUT THE AUTHOR

Scott Pavelle is an attorney and a noted professional storyteller. A past president of the StorySwap storytelling guild, his repertoire of over 150 works includes both traditional and original pieces of all kinds, and ranges from children's stories to ghost stories and of course the occasional romance of high adventure. His short stories have been published in both foreign-language school textbooks and anthologies.

His other interests include exceptional cooking skills ("A book based on our annual holiday cookie extravaganza has to be the next project up"), field mycology ("Check out my online Bolete Filter"), in-depth football articles ("Yes, I'm the one responsible for the BTSC Steeler Big Boards"), and a reading obsession that dates back to the age of four.

A well-travelled native New Yorker, he shares his Pittsburgh home with a wife, two daughters, and a brand new puppy. Find out more about Scott at his website:

www.pavellelaw.com

www.ingramcontent.com/pod-product-compliance
Lightning Source LLC
Chambersburg PA
CBHW061138170626
46809CB00003B/901